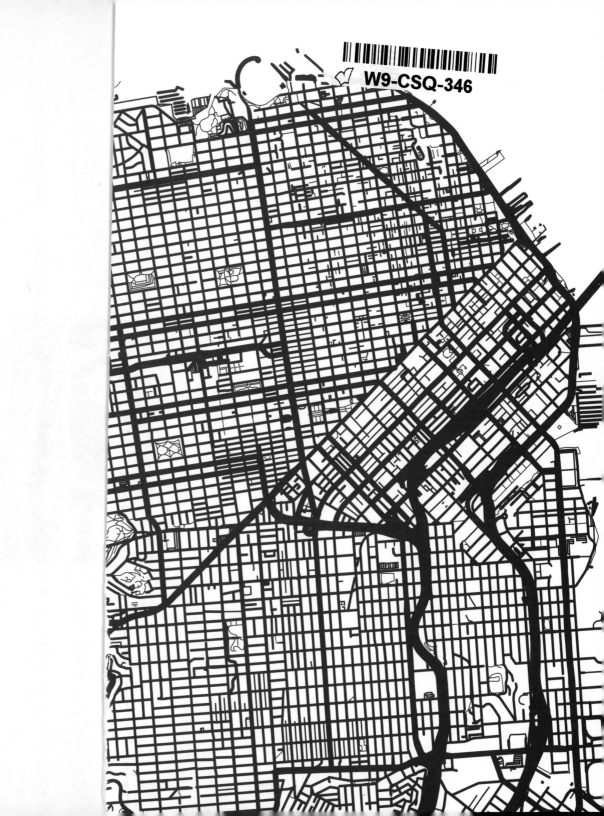

SHINE U

TOMORI

SHINE UNTIL TOMORROW

CARLA MALDEN

RARE BIRD BOOKS
LOS ANGELES, CALIF.

Rare Bird Books
453 South Spring Street, Suite 302
Los Angeles, CA 90013
rarebirdlit.com

Set in Berling LT
Printed in the United States

10 9 8 7 6 5 4 3 2 1

Library of Congress Cataloging-in-Publication Data

Names: Malden, Carla, author.
Title: Shine Until Tomorrow / by Carla Malden.
Description: Los Angeles, CA : Rare Bird Books, [2020] I Audience: Ages
Teens. I Audience: Grades 10-12.
Identifiers: LCCN 2020014066 I ISBN 9781644281420 (hardback)
Subjects: CYAC: Self actualization (Psychology)—Fiction. I Time
travel—Fiction. I Bands (Music)—Fiction. I Love—Fiction. I Family
life—California, Northern—Fiction. I California—Fiction. I California—
History—Fiction.
Classification: LCC PZ7.1.M346953 Shi 2020 I
DDC [Fic]—dc23

LC record available at https://lccn.loc.gov/2020014066

Yes, my guard stood hard when abstract threats too noble to neglect
Deceived me into thinking I had something to protect
Good and bad, I define these terms quite clear, no doubt, somehow
Ah, but I was so much older then I'm younger than that now

Bob Dylan

CHAPTER
1

THE DREAM is always the same. Every time. Speeding through dense fog. Foot stomping brake. Car galloping, careening through mist. Zero visibility. Then it appears—the Golden Gate Bridge. Stomping on brake. Again. Again. Nothing. Only acceleration. Bridge looms closer. Distance distorts, some weird parallax. Suddenly, a curtain of fog obscures everything. Airless. Suffocating. Jerking the steering wheel, but the car remains out of control. On the bridge now, speeding faster and faster. Flashes of the city slice through the fog. It should be getting closer, but it keeps receding into the distance, always a little too far to reach. And there's one more thing. The bridge doesn't extend far enough. No reaching the other side. Telescoping in— faster, closer, faster, closer. The car flies off the edge. Ocean rushes up. Car plummets down, down. Crashes through the surface. Smack.

That's when I wake up. Every time. In the sliver of air that hangs over the bay. In that split second before the whoosh of water. In that last breath. I bolt upright, gasping. My hair sticks to the back of my neck, glued with sweat. My heart pounds in my temples. My throat is dry, like I swallowed a cotton ball, a wad of cotton balls. Thank God it's just a dream. *The* dream—the one I've had ever since I realized that, someday, I was going to have to drive a car. I flop back down, sink into my pillow, reach for my phone, killing the alarm before it has a chance to go off. The date on the screen reminds me—last day of school. So where's that summer feeling?

I drag myself through my morning routine. It's a whirlwind (I say facetiously) of checking texts and emails, punctuated by the obligatory teeth-brushing and face-washing. Mom bought me some new face wash containing not one, not two, but three different kinds of acid. It boasts about them right there on the front of the bottle. Mom says you can't start taking care of your skin too soon. And, oh yes, don't forget your neck. Be sure to moisturize your neck. That's one of those things she wants me to learn from her mistakes; she neglected her neck and there's simply no backtracking. Apparently, a neck neglected is a neck permanently creased. I cannot project into a future where I worry about my neck, but I use the new face wash because it smells like grapefruit. For some inexplicable reason, the smell provides me with a good minute or so of optimism about the day.

Optimism quickly dashed by a look in the mirror. There's something about the way my features come together that's disheartening. They don't. Come together, that is. My face is round, but my nose is long. My mouth is wide, but my upper lip is thin. And my forehead is too high. You could only describe my hair as no-color brown. The last time I got it cut, which was at least a year ago, the haircutter told me that highlights would make a world of difference, give me a whole new outlook. I didn't bother to explain that highlights could never be up to that task. My general physiognomy is a study in mismatchedness, facial Mad Libs. Whatever.

I check my phone again. Not that I ever get anything worth mentioning—just the usual spam and a text from Sarah about some stupid party tonight. She thinks it might be fun, as though the two of us could ever have anything remotely resembling a good time at a party with all the kids from school. Why would we want to put ourselves through that kind of torture? After all, we have the entire school day to luxuriate in the feeling (again, facetiously) that we're from a different planet from everyone else. It's not exactly a feeling you want to extend beyond its mandatory 8:30-3:00 parameters. Sarah may be my only true friend in that place, but sometimes she has really lame ideas.

I run a brush through my hair. It's still a little damp at the nape of my neck from sweating my way through the bridge dream. I yank on a pair of black leggings and a black T-shirt. Where is it written a person has to wear sherbet colors just because it's June? I head for the kitchen.

My mother has already left for work. She must be showing that house over in Ross and wants to make the place look perfect, like no real people have ever actually lived there. I sit at the breakfast table and pick at a slightly burnt oatmeal cookie. My mother baked a batch last night to set out at the open house. She'll stick them in the oven at the Ross "property" for a few minutes before the prospective buyers arrive so that the house will smell like cinnamon. Realtor tricks. My mom knows them all. She put too much cinnamon in these. They have a weird aftertaste that prickles the back of my tongue.

I wash it away with a swig of coffee. My mom left a pot, nearly full. I pour some into a mug, the one I gave my mom for Mother's Day when I was seven. I had it made at one of those kiosks on the wharf where they take your picture and it ends up on the lid of a heart-shaped ceramic box or on a plate or a mug or something. I keep thinking I'll develop a taste for black coffee one of these days because that's the way my dad drinks it. I like the visual of black coffee in a thick white mug—just the way my dad likes it—but the taste for straight black hasn't kicked in yet, so I add milk. Lots of milk. I prefer soy, but we're out. It's kind of weird to watch my little kid self rise toward me as I raise the mug to my lips.

My lips are a little chapped even though I sanded them last night with a toothbrush. I read in some magazine that gently brushing your lips with a dry toothbrush is a good way to exfoliate them. Good idea to keep your lips kissable at all times, the article said. I'm definitely not about to require kissability any time soon. But for some reason, I decided to take the dry toothbrush method for a test drive. I had nothing better to do at 11:30 on a Thursday night, the last night of junior year. It's a pain to have to do all those things that keep a person smooth and silky, but I do them anyway because you never know. I mean, I kind of really do know, but you never one-hundred-percent know when you might wish your body was, at the very least, not all stubbly or flakey-lipped. I'm presuming this might be a worry in my semi-near future as opposed to the far distant future of the saggy neck, but I repeat: unlikely.

I pick up a flyer for a four-bedroom with a pool. My mom left a stack of them on the table. She keeps saying she'll make a killing if she can find a buyer for the place. A killing—seriously. The copy is full of phrases like "the coveted flats of Kentfield" and "exceptional indoor-outdoor flow." I think the place looks butt-heinous in the photo, like someone stuck a false Shakespearean front onto the Brady Bunch house. But what do I know about Northern California real estate?

I toss the paper aside and pick up my copy of "America's Best Colleges." I leave the book there, on the kitchen table, because I eat alone a lot of the time and it sort of keeps me company. I know that's weird, but when I leaf through the pages, it's not exactly like I pretend I'm there in the library at Oberlin or at an a cappella concert at Williams—I mean, it's not quite that pathetic—but it does take my mind off of life as it is in the here and now. If briefly.

When Sarah and I were little, like in elementary school, we used to play this game we called "college." Fairly self-explanatory. It was like playing house, but it was us being in college—having boyfriends, going to parties, that kind of thing. Being egghead kids, our actual favorite part was creating our class schedules. I guess when I look through "America's Best," it's like playing college again. But for real…or real at one remove…or what will be real if I can make it through one more year.

Multicolored Post-its poke out all through the book. But it's the entry marked by the single orange Post-it at the end that I read over and over. Almost like a tic, or to be strictly accurate, a compulsion. I've never technically been diagnosed or anything, but I probably do have a little OCD when it comes to certain things, this college book being a prime example. The orange Post-it is stuck on Yale. I know, like me. Rimshot, please. I'm applying Early Decision to Yale. I mentally rewrite my essay every night as I'm falling asleep. (Some people count sheep; I count extra-curriculars.) In a few more months, I'll be sending it in. I don't know how I'll fall asleep after that.

My college counselor thinks I actually have a decent chance. She let slip that more than one of my teachers has said I'm too smart for my own good. I think she meant it nicely—a left-handed compliment. Or a right-handed insult depending on how you look at it. But the truth is, being smart is the only thing I've ever been halfway good at. It doesn't require any fundamental interpersonal skills like the ability to make small talk or hide what you're really thinking. When you think about it, in terms of human beingness, it's actually the easiest thing to be good at. That's the thing about Yale, or at least my well-refined vision of Yale: since I'm basically biding my time by waiting to get there, I picture it as a place full of other people who've also been biding their time waiting to get there to meet people like me.

I grab my camera off the counter and hang it around my neck. It's a vintage Leica, a hefty piece of equipment—so anti-digital—and the weight of the thing makes me feel a little more like I have a reason to exist. Sometimes when it's hanging around my neck, I run my hand over its surface. It's got this great texture. I don't know exactly what it's made of, but the feel of it—sort of pebbly, like alligator hide—connects me with my father and his father before him. One, I never knew; he died before I was born. The other, I hardly ever see anymore. The world around me is completely different from the world that was around each of them when they were my age, but I get to look at it through the same lens.

✧✧

Even though we are mere hours away from summer vacation, the Marin County fog has settled over school. It has found its way into all the crevices, nestling between buildings and blanketing the expanses of grass, like it's staking its claim on summer. I don't mind. I like the cool morning air. Besides, it's easier to get a good shot when it's overcast. Photography is all about light, really, and clouds filter the sunlight, softening contrast and shadows. Sometimes when I take a picture on a gray day and look at it later, I see details I never saw in person. Like magic.

I plop myself down on a bench and pull my legs up under me to wait for the first bell to ring. I raise my camera to my eye and scan for a decent shot. A banner is stretched across the quad: "Congratulations Class of 2007!" Three kids sit beneath it—two girls and a guy. One girl is jabbering on her phone. The other is texting on her BlackBerry, thumbs moving like the wings of a hummingbird. The guy communes with his Game Boy, jerking his upper body in sync with the zap of a laser or the slaying of a medieval monster. I snap the tableau. Click.

Over by the lunch table, several of our award-winning cheerleaders are signing each other's yearbooks.

14

They hand them back to one another with air kisses. I snap their picture. Click.

A smiley guy in a basketball jersey struts across the quad, one bicep-sculpted arm slung over his girlfriend. Corey-and-Cassidy. Every school has their Corey-and-Cassidy couple, I bet. They've been a thing all year, but she still looks up at him with what appears to be unadulterated adoration. He slam dunks his textbooks into a trashcan. Click.

I can't help but eavesdrop on a gaggle of my classmates. It's okay. When I've got my camera up to my eye, I'm invisible. You might say it's one of the major perks of being the photography nerd, though many in my class might argue that invisibility is one of my salient features, camera or no camera.

Vanessa is the leader of the pack. She turns to Amanda who's been trailing her like a puppy hoping for a treat since about eighth grade. Rachel and Kelly are just happy to be cool-girl-adjacent.

Amanda's eyes go wide. "Matthew Wilson alert," she says.

"Who cares?" says Vanessa. "He's got major commitment issues. I can't believe I was so obsessed with him."

Even so, she checks her reflection in Kelly's mirrored sunglasses and flips her hair out from where it was tucked behind her ear. She cocks her head so that a few strands sweep down over one eye. Click.

Turns out they saw me after all. Amanda looks straight into my lens and flips me off. With a perfectly polished nail, Tahitian Aqua or something. I can feel the heat rush to my face as I look away. I know my cheeks must have gone all blotchy magenta, my personal hallmark of broadcasting humiliation. I can't do anything about it. I have no control over my autonomic nervous system. All I can do is pretend I didn't notice Amanda's little gesture.

The girly-girls saunter over to me. I busy myself by fiddling with the lens on my camera so that I'm the very soul of nonchalance by the time they're standing there next to me.

"Hey, Mari," says Rachel. "Are you going to the party tonight?" She doesn't mean it sarcastically. Even though she's part of this group, Rachel has basic niceness in her DNA.

"Well," I say, "I never actually received an epistolary notice, so in keeping with customary social convention, which God knows I strive to do at every possible turn, I will not be in attendance." I do that sometimes—just launch full-throttle into a crazy word thing. Weirdly, it's easier for me than a simple "yes" or "no." I've known these girls since middle school. I was paired with Amanda to build a cross-section of a volcano in sixth grade. I did a dramatic recitation of Coleridge's "Xanadu" with Kelly in World Lit. I was Vanessa's lab partner in Bio. But when they're in a clump, a congealed mass of conditioned hair and skinny jeans, they make me feel like it's the first day of kindergarten. And then I pull out every fifty-cent word I know and toss them all together—like a make-your-own scramble on a breakfast menu. I'm not proud of it, but I'm also not going to lie. It makes me feel better to see the looks on their faces go from blank to blanker. It reminds me that if I can just hang in there, I'll be out of this place and end up in a place (Yale or, God forbid, a Yale runner-up) where there might be a few more people like me.

Sure enough: Vanessa crinkles up her face to make sense of my nonsense, but gives up. "See you later," she says. And they're off.

Just then Sarah appears. "What did they want with the likes of you?"

I'm not insulted. It's a perfectly legitimate question.

"Just to torment me," I say. "About that party tonight."

Sarah sits next to me on the bench and starts braiding her hair. She thinks a braid camouflages the frizzies, which she abhors, but when her hair is braided, the ends stick out even more and actually emphasize the frizz. I would never tell her though.

"You didn't answer my texts" she says. "I think we should go. To the party."

"Why?"

"I don't know," Sarah shrugs. "Maybe kind of like a sociological study."

"No, thanks," I say. "Not I. Anyway, my father's got me this weekend so the point is, shall we say, moot. You go ahead, Margaret Mead."

"She's anthropology," Sarah says.

"Point: Sarah," I say.

"Thank you very much."

"Besides, parties are against my religion." Sarah mouths along as I say that. She's heard it before. More than once.

"You know what, Mari?" Sarah says. "Sometimes you can really let the air out of the old exuberance balloon."

"My specialty," I say. "My calling."

It's true: knee-jerk negativity is my default setting. But Sarah has been my tell-everything-to person since third grade, so I owe her something a little more last-day-of-school celebratory. "At least we have three months of freedom to look forward to," I add.

"I know!" Sarah says. "And then seniors! Can you believe it?"

"I can. We've been waiting long enough. But that makes this our crucial summer. I've got to clock some major community service hours. Did I tell you I found this program where I can kill two birds, proverbially speaking, with one stone? You know how I was agonizing between the old and the young—you know, as service-worthy populations—so I found this place where I'm going to…air quote—facilitate interaction—between little kids and old people. And

I signed up for that poetry workshop at the hippie-dippie bookstore. With any luck, they'll locate my inner Sylvia Plath so I can attach a poetic gem to my application. And I've got that internship at the Bio Med lab. Maybe I'll isolate a genome or something."

"Fingers crossed," says Sarah, and she holds up both hands with all digits crossed. She's making fun of me, of course, but I happen to know that her summer doesn't look much different. And then she adds, "We are so digging ourselves deeper and deeper into the heart of dorkness."

I laugh. No one does the smart-funny literary mash-up like Sarah Hampton.

"Maybe we should give ourselves one week to do nothing. Just one week to, I don't know, go to the beach," Sarah suggests.

"A week is seven whole days," I remind her.

"So I've been told," says Sarah. "Also known as: just seven days, a mere seven days, only seven days."

We mosey from the quad over to the Humanities Building. Our school is relatively new. Even though it has all these Northern California greener-than-thou features, it looks a lot like a Palm Springs motel. Two-story buildings ringed with balconies. Overhangs shield the outdoor walkways. It took me a while to get used to the stairs. They're the kind without risers and I used to feel like I was going to fall through the gaping holes between them, even though I couldn't possibly. Still, the sensation of seeing air between the steps, or worse, people milling around below, was very disconcerting. Thankfully and, I might add, remarkably, I'm okay with them now, which is a lucky thing because our homeroom is on the second floor.

Mr. Chappell is already taking stuff down from the bulletin board. To remind us that he's the cool teacher (again, resorting to the heaviest of air quotes), he eschews the dress code today, wearing cargo shorts and a tie-dyed T-shirt. A ratty thing that must be left over from the birth of tie-dye itself. Mr. Chappell is old enough to have stuff like that lying around. Once, on the day before Thanksgiving, he wore a T-shirt with the logo of some ancient band on it. He seemed genuinely disappointed—"crestfallen" would be the word—when no one had ever heard of them. He said we were making him feel old. Straight line if I ever heard one.

Sarah and I slide into our seats. Everybody's talking—last day of school and all—so we just keep talking, too. "The point is," I say. "When I go for my Yale interview, they're not really going to care if I have a tan."

Mr. Chappell yelps as his thumb meets the wrong end of a pushpin.

Sarah leans in close to me and whispers, "I'm adding Kenyon to my list. I read that sixty-eight percent of the kids there meet their future spouses. Spice."

"Cardamom," I say.

"Turmeric perhaps?" says Sarah. We go a few more rounds, but Sarah is intent on making a point.

"It's not like I want to get married or anything," she says adamantly. "Not for like the next fifteen years, I mean, duh. I just thought it might be fun to have a boyfriend…you know, for a change."

"Who needs the aggravation?" I say. "I mean, look around you."

We do a quick sweep of the room. It is kind of a sorry batch of guys. Actually, Alex Shay isn't bad. He looks like someone you would want to know—when he smiles, that is, which is pretty often. He smiled at me once, right at me, and I was so stunned that it took me a few minutes to realize I didn't smile back. Some neural pathway just froze. I wanted a do-over, but we never happened to be looking directly at each other again. Just as well, because right now I catch him, out of my peripheral vision, uncoiling a paper clip and using the sharp end to scratch the inside of his ear. Who needs that brand of gross?

"Res ipsa loquitur," I say.

"Okay," Sarah says, "so I didn't take Latin."

"The thing speaks for itself. Besides, let's just say for the sake of argument that you find someone, it's just a ticket on the fast train to Heartbreak Town."

"You've been reading too much Raymond Chandler," says Sarah.

Mr. Chappell perches on the edge of his desk and claps his hands like he is trying to rally a roomful of preschoolers.

"Okay, teeners," he says, "let's settle. I know your agile little minds are already out the door, but first, some party favors." He pulls a stack of report cards out of his leather notebook—a splotched, battered thing with acorns and vines hand-tooled all over it. Everyone groans in unison. I pull my trusty old calculator out of my backpack. My dad works in tech and wrangled this new iPhone thing for me a couple weeks in advance of its release on the world, but I don't trust its calculator function. All I need is for there to be a hidden bug undetected in beta. My GPA is programmed into my calculator, at the ready: 4.2

Mr. Chappell strolls the room, handing out report cards. "I just want to say—have a great summer. You're kids and it's summertime. What could be cooler?"

Sarah rolls her eyes. Isn't it just so lame when some teacher type wants to let you know he can still identify with the whole teen experience?

"Get out there and peg the old fun meter," Mr. Chappell continues as he weaves through the desks. "And remember, life is not a dress rehearsal." How cute—a little nugget of Dr. Phil wisdom.

It's like he's serving up a whole combo platter of excitement, anticipation and pride when he hands me my grades. I enter them into my calculator one by one. A string of 4.0's. Extra points for acing AP English Lit. and AP Calc.

"What?!" says Sarah. "Windham gave me a B-minus in Spanish. What's up with that?"

"You should have taken Latin."

"I kind of wanted to take a language people speak. Like people who are alive. In the past many centuries. Millenia."

Sarah is talking to me but I'm not paying attention. It's embarrassing to admit, but I'm too absorbed in the galaxy of my own GPA. All that's left is Photography. Mr. Chappell's class. I start to punch in another 4.0, but then I see it: "Incomplete." I don't understand. I actually run my finger along the word to make sure I'm reading it properly. He must have made a mistake. I mean, I did every single assignment, feeble though some of them may have been. Always turned them in on time, even when I had an AP Calc test the same day and was up studying all night. I stare at the word—Incomplete—trying to make sense of it. Everybody else is gathering up their things, shoving their yearbooks under Mr. Chappell's nose for him to sign, then charging out of the room into summer. And I sit there, staring at the Incomplete.

Finally, I walk up to his desk. "Mr. Chappell," I say haltingly, "I think you made a mistake here. You gave me an Incomplete."

"Oh yeah, Mari, I wanted to talk to you about that."

"I can't have an Incomplete on my transcript. I'm applying Early Decision to Yale. I've spent my entire high school career constructing the perfect application. Middle school, too, actually. Fourth grade science project…" I'm seeing my academic life pass before my eyes, which, in fact, are pooling with tears. I swallow hard. "An Incomplete will slaughter me," I manage to say.

Mr. Chappell looks at me in that nauseating way that teachers do to show you they sincerely understand you. "Take a deep breath," he says. "Everything's going to be fine."

"But the thing is…I did every assignment. I did every extra credit project…" I swallow again. Really hard. I do not want to cry. I know that it's a stupid reason to cry and not exactly the epitome of maturity, but I can feel that hot, stinging pressure of inevitability building behind my eyeballs. "I thought they were all pretty good," I say, indignant.

"Better than pretty good," he says.

So what's going on here? I think. *Huh?* "Photography's kind of my thing," I say. My voice cracks. Just when I thought I was pulling it together.

"You have talent. That's why I'm not going to let you get away with that final portrait assignment."

"What do you mean? You're telling me I'm getting an Incomplete because I'm good at this?"

"Let me see your camera," Mr. Chappell says.

I remove the Leica from around my neck and hand it over. Mr. Chappell takes it with loving care, examines it. "Quite the piece of machinery."

"My father gave it to me. It was his father's."

"It's got history," says Mr. Chappell.

I nod. *Just tell me whatever I have to do to make it so it's like this stupid Incomplete never happened.* I'm begging him silently. Telepathically imploring him. "I reiterate," I say, "you're telling me I did such a good job the rest of the semester that I'm being penalized?"

"Something like that," he says, unphased. He unscrews the telephoto lens. "This lens," he says. "It puts too much distance between you and your subject. When I look at your portrait assignment, it feels like you were an observer."

"That's what photography is," I manage. "Observing."

He shakes his head, smiling like he's got a secret. *No. Apparently that's not what photography is.* He opens the bottom drawer of his desk, pulls out another lens and screws it onto my camera. "For a portrait to be really great," he says, "you need to connect with your subject. Get to know them. Look inside them. Be close. Not just with the camera, but you know, emotionally."

Suddenly, I wish I'd signed up for Printmaking as my Art elective. I bet Mrs. Fletcher doesn't care about communing with the paper.

"I'll do it today," I promise.

"No," he says. "Take your time. You have all summer."

"I don't want all summer. I'm going to fix this right away."

"Mari…" Mr. Chappell gives me that out-from-under-the-eyelids forced empathy look again. "Take a deep breath. It's not about getting anything fixed. It's about taking the picture I know you're capable of."

"How will I know if it's good enough?" I ask.

"You'll know," says Mr. Chappell. And he hands me back the camera.

CHAPTER

2

KENTFIELD IS the kind of place where you can ride your bike and not feel like a total freak. As I pedal down the street, I try to remind myself that people come here to look at the natural beauty, even though that's hard to remember when it's just your regular personal neighborhood. Anyway, there are always tourists renting bikes and tooling around, having picnics and getting lost. Of course, there are a fair number of green types who bicycle to work. The city government people—Chamber of Commerce and all that—are always promoting Bike to Work Day. Way more than once a year, it seems. I don't get how people can be so into causes like that. If every single person in Kentfield rides a bike to work one day, who cares? If every single person in all of Marin County rides a bike to work one day—really, what would that do for the planet? But at least the whole save-the-earth thing gives me a convenient excuse for riding my bike. I've avoided the driver's license issue for a year now. Statistics show more and more kids putting off getting their license. Unfortunately, where I live, that doesn't seem to be the case. I try to think of myself as a trendsetter, but the trend's not catching on in Kentfield.

The jacarandas are blooming. They shed like crazy, dropping their indigo blossoms everywhere. Every year I forget how slippery they are. I pedal extra carefully as I turn onto my driveway; as many petals are strewn on the ground as left hanging on the trees. I used to help my father sweep them away, even though we knew we could never keep up with them. But he doesn't live here anymore, so I just bicycle over them.

The driveway has an uphill slant. You can't really see it; even so, I've come to associate burning quads with arriving home.

Inside the house, I make a beeline for the fridge and pull out a Diet Coke. I pop the top and drink about half the can while I listen to voicemail on my mother's old-fashioned answering machine. I can't believe my mother still uses this clunky, old thing—so lame—but she insists it's more reliable than cell Voicemail. Of course, she only says that because she always screws up when she tries to retrieve her messages from her BlackBerry. Somehow they evaporate into the wireless black hole with which my mother has a close personal relationship.

"In my business," my mom says, "I can't afford to be missing calls."

There had been no business for my mother before the divorce. Like a lot of moms in the area, she used to be the stay-at-home variety, but now you'd think she'd been selling real estate forever. The zeal of the convert. Who knew she had a hidden knack for finding the just-right house for people, like a one-woman match.com of house-hunting?

I open the freezer and pull out a carton of vanilla Häagen-Dazs, scoop a heaping spoonful and take a lick. I let the ice cream melt in my mouth while I slurp some more Coke. An on-demand, in-the-mouth float. So much easier than going to the trouble of actually making one in a glass.

The first message is from my mom's boyfriend, Patrick. They work at the same real estate agency. "Hi, Diana."

Patrick must have big news because his voice squeaks when he gets excited. Once I told him he could have had a big career as the voice of a cartoon. He didn't take it well. I was only trying to make conversation, which is always a bit of a challenge, to put it mildly, when my mom's not in the room. When it's just two of us, old Patrick and me, you might say silence reigns supreme.

There's more. "I just got that Oakmont listing." (I knew it—big news.) "We'll celebrate this weekend. I'm psyched. Maybe I'll upgrade our room to deluxe!" He pronounces it dee-loox, which makes me gag on my ice cream a little. Not to mention, picturing my mom in a dee-loox hotel room with Patrick.

The next message begins. It's my dad. "Di, it's me…Listen…" I barely have to listen to the rest. Any message that begins that way will end with my father flaking out on the weekend. He's done that a lot lately. "Something's come up. I can't take Mari this weekend. I'm in the middle of this damn crisis at work…" So much for watching *On The Waterfront* together Saturday night. That's sort of our thing—watching old movies together. But between work and the new girlfriend, a good-sized crack has opened up in my dad's life—turns out it's just the right size for me to fall into. That's the thing about divorce that parents don't get. Once they get together with a new significant other, you're just a satellite orbiting their shiny new planet. Doesn't mean they don't want to have you touch down every now and then, but if the timing doesn't work out just right for a link-up, there's always the next rotation.

My dad keeps going. "I know I've missed a few, but I'll take her for a couple in a row."

The ice cream goes sour in my mouth. I swallow hard, turn on the tap and stick my mouth under to wash away the taste.

My phone rings. My ringtone is the theme song from *I Love Lucy*. I know all about the sociopolitical theses purporting that Ricky kept Lucy under his thumb, not letting her perform in his nightclub shows, but I chose the ringtone because it reminds me of when I was a little girl and had to stay home, sick, from school. There was always a *Lucy* to be found. Before I knew that Ricky was stifling Lucy's creativity, I just laughed when Lucy shoved chocolates down her candy factory uniform or flitted around saying, "It's a moo-moo!" while she pretended to be a Martian.

"Hi Sarah," I answer, wandering through the house. "I'm home for the weekend."

"Cool," says Sarah. Then she catches herself. "I mean, I'm sorry. I know you haven't seen your dad for a while."

"It's okay." Thank goodness Sarah knows it's really not okay, so that I don't have to say that out loud.

"So...if you're going to be home..."

I know what's coming next. She's going to bring up the party. "We'll go," I say. No need for the whole back-and-forth. "And we'll dance like nobody's watching." It's an in-joke. One of those self-help things people say about how to live your best life. We read it in a magazine a few years ago and then spent the next hour outdoing each other with demonstrations of what dancing like nobody's watching would look like. It was pretty funny. We've been saying it ever since.

"I better go," says Sarah. "I have to find something to wear."

"Let's get there late and leave early," I say, suddenly sorry I agreed.

"Deal," she says.

I head down the hall toward the bedrooms. The walls are covered with family photos framed in honey-colored wood. They're hung in clusters of three or five because my mother read somewhere that items should always be grouped in odd numbers. After the divorce, she didn't take down the ones with my dad in them. I was never sure if that was because she didn't want me to feel like he'd been erased from my life or because she didn't want to create even-numbered groupings.

I don't usually look at the pictures, but for some reason, today they catch my eye. One in particular. I must be about three years old in this photograph, but all you can see of me is a bit of my neck and the corner of my wide-open mouth because my head is thrown back in laughter. Both my parents, one on each side of me, are tickling me. They look as happy as I do. You can see their whole faces—not like mine—and they look downright blissful. And the thing is, even though they're tickling me, they're looking at each other. Right into each other's eyes over my thrown-back, laughing face. I wonder how people could look at each other like that one day, and then some other day, ten, eleven years later, just not feel like looking at each other at all anymore.

I'm sure my mother must have read a book on how to break the separation news to your kid. I'm not sure if the dialogue was lifted from a scene in a movie or if it just felt that way. The whole scene, in fact , felt more movie than real life—the three of us out to dinner at a restaurant just fancy enough that no one would be tempted to raise their voice. Especially me. The big take-away was: "This has nothing to do with you."

"Nothing at all," my father added.

Craziest thing ever. I knew what they meant, of course. Not my fault. I knew that. Even believed it. But nothing to do with me? Come on...it had everything to do with me. How could something that was going to make a person's life never ever be the same have nothing to do with that person? How could two people who looked at each other like my parents looked at each other in that photograph just give up? Once, I asked my mother that very question, and she told me that someday I would understand. But frankly, I'm not sure I want to.

You're supposed to want your parents to be happy, but in my albeit limited experience, you want them to be happy *as parents*, not as ex-parents. A mother going out on dates in a little black cocktail dress...a father succumbing to the cliché of having a girlfriend young enough to be your older sister—much older, but still within the mathematical realm of possibility...giant ugh.

I pass the family photos and wander into my mother's room, wondering what to wear to the party. I know I can't compete with the girly-girls. I'll never have on exactly the right anything, and I'm not very adept at selecting items of clothing that look like they belong together, but since, as of an hour ago, I'm a high school senior, I figure I might as well try to rummage up an outfit that surpasses my usual sartorial study in aggressively not caring.

My mom's room is all dove gray and white, designed to be slumber serene. She has a huge walk-in closet—a professional closet organizer had her way with it, so that my mom's work suits are color coded, even though they're all beige, navy, and black. A row of white blouses hangs above them. She wears one of them in her official realtor photo, which smiles—a frozen, toothy smile—from the back of bus benches all over town. Positively mortifying.

On the other side of the closet are color-coordinated sweat suits. Most of them are Juicy brand. One is even hot pink. If that doesn't scream desperate attempt to recapture long-lost youth, I don't know what does. It crosses my mind that I could wear that pink number to the party—ironically, of course. But no.

I'm giving the tops one last scan when something on a high shelf catches my eye. The tip of a sleeve hanging down, something delicate and gauzy. I stretch to reach, but can't make it. I stand on tiptoe. Still can't reach. I jump a few times, finally manage to make contact, and tug. An avalanche of boxes and assorted stuff tumbles down—all the junk my mom has shoved up there that would make the closet lady cringe. I deflect the onslaught with my arms (that one misguided year playing soccer in elementary school finally paying off).

At least the filmy top drifted down with all the junk. It's a floral print—sheer, but not completely see-through. Several inches of paisley ring the hem. Maybe if I wear it, Sarah won't give me a hard time for not even trying. There's the faintest ting-a-ling when I pull it over my head. It comes from these tiny bells that dangle from the ties around the open neck and from where the sleeves billow at the wrists.

Shoeboxes landed helter-skelter, spewing their contents: random photos, old receipts, and shoes. Tons of shoes. There is also a scrapbook, covered in faded fabric and threadbare around the edges. When I open it, a few loose buttons fall out. The kind you pin on your shirt to let the world know where you stand, or that people used to anyway. "Peace Now." "Make Love Not War." "Fly Translove Airways." Give me a break.

Taped to the first page of the book is a wreath of flowers, long dried nearly to dust. My mom could not have worn this thing! There are ticket stubs to concerts at the Fillmore Auditorium. The Grateful Dead. Jefferson Airplane. Quicksilver Messenger Service. Country Joe and the Fish. Strings of colored beads. Oh-my-God, more bona fide relics—what delusional flower children vomitously called "love beads."

I flip through the pages as though I'm on an archaeological dig and come across a snapshot of two teenagers—a guy and a girl kissing. Another photo shows they are two among what must be hundreds of people, maybe more. A crowd of bodies, shoulder to shoulder, hip to hip, bleeds off the torn edge of the photograph. My father must have shot this. He probably carried his camera, our camera, around like I do now and snapped all the weirdness around him. He must have felt like I did when he was a teenager—separate and separated.

I study the photograph for comparisons in our style. What does Mr. Chappell know anyway? Then I notice: my father didn't take the picture. He's in the picture…with my mother. I lean down closer to the book splayed open on the pearl-gray carpet, lower my face to inches away, squinting at it through the years. That *is* my mother and father kissing! My mother's hair hangs so far down her back, you can't see where it ends in the frame. A lens flare looks like a special effect, like the sun sparked when they kissed.

I keep turning the pages, compelled to see more. My father in bell-bottoms and a fringed vest with hair down to his shoulders. My mother dancing in a field with a painted daisy winding its way up her cheek, its petals encircling her right eye. The two of them grinning as they flash peace signs. Shit. My white-collar parents were blue denim hippies. How is that possible? Sure, my mother bought the director's cut of *Woodstock*, but who knew it was a personal flashback?

I turn the page again. There's the yellowing paper sleeve of a 45 rpm record. My dad once told me they were called "singles." The picture on the paper jacket is of four guys and a girl. Like in all the pictures so far, there's a lot of blue jean, a lot of beads, a lot of hair. Hippies. How clichéd. It crosses my mind that a cliché might require the passage of time, but then I realize that I know plenty of people living a cliché in real time. Neon Dream—that's the name of the band. The song: *Tamara Moonlight.*

I'm pretty sure I've heard of that song. A few notes come to me, a snatch of melody, then the chorus filters through a door in my brain that's slightly ajar. Of course! Now I remember. My father used to sing me that song every night when I was little, in that half-asleep moment between the last bedtime story and lights out.

"What on earth happened here?" My mother's voice makes me jump.

I hold up the scrapbook for her to see. "What on earth happened *here*?" I brandish the book as though it were contaminated. "I mean, I guess I knew you were around in the sixties, but I didn't know you were so…sixties!"

"I forgot about this old thing," my mom says. "I used to want to remember everything that happened. Every moment seemed so important," she adds, in a way you could only call "wistful," and and I would never before have described my mom as "wistful." Not in my entire life.

"Did you look through it?" she says, as though it were something super personal like a diary. She takes it out of my hands and her whole face changes.

"You never told me you had such a sordid past," I say, only half-joking.

"It hardly qualifies as sordid."

"Free love, naked parties…mind altering substances," I say. "Oh yeah, that qualifies."

"It wasn't like that."

I shoot her a look.

"Okay," she says, shrugging. "Maybe it was like that for some people. I'm not saying I happened to be one of them. Anyway, that was a million years ago. It was a whole other world." She looks off into the middle distance as though that world were hanging out there, if only she could focus on the right plane. "A better world in a lot of ways."

"All you need is love, huh?" I say.

"Something like that."

"Well," I say, "all you got is the house." I'm sorry I said it the minute it comes out of my mouth. Must have been all that scrutinizing the family gallery— ripped the scab off the last several years of my parents' split. Proving my point—I am a living, breathing clichéd child of divorce. Pathetic.

"I went through nine years of fertility treatments for this abuse," my mom says, more to herself than to me.

"On behalf of medical science, I apologize." I mean it to be a joke, but it comes out snarky. I remove the

45 from the scrapbook and show it to my mom, a peace offering. "Look at this. My special song."

"It was our song first," she says. "Dad's and mine."

"You had a song?"

"Of course we had a song. When you're young and in love, you have a song."

I don't quite know what to make of this. Young. In love. My parents. Brain circuit frizzle.

"He left a message by the way. Dad. Alert the media. He's busy this weekend." Even though I'm perversely fascinated with this treasure trove of a scrapbook, I don't want to think about my parents and their misspent youth right now. Not after Mr. Chappell's Incomplete. It's too much for one day. Anxiety overload. Besides, I'm not sure it's a good idea for my mom to go burrowing into her past. Once, about a year ago, she came across an anniversary card my dad had given her. She had slid it into her copy of *The Tipping Point* to keep her place. The card was still there when she went zooming through one of her semi-annual white tornado purges. That card landed her in bed for the rest of the afternoon, and it took several more days before she was back on the terra firma of business suits and real estate sales. So I leave the scrapbook behind and head down the hall to the kitchen. My mother's voice trails after, "I'm sorry..."

She follows me into the kitchen. She shakes her head when she spots the ice cream container left out on the counter, but puts it back in the freezer without scolding me. Then she shakes her head again. "I don't know what's wrong with that man. He can never think of anyone but himself. This really ruins my plans." And in one fell swoop, she's back to the present, peace-and-love scrapbook memories banished.

"Oh yeah," I say. "Patrick called, too. He's psyched for your weekend." I nail the gung-ho in how he said "pysched," then mime gagging myself, finger down throat. Juvenile but effective.

"Well, I can't go now," Mom says. "I'm not going to leave you alone."

"I'll be fine. Go. Have fun." I dig my camera out of my backpack, start snapping pictures of my mom. "Besides, I won't be alone. Sarah and I are going to a party."

At first, my mom is kind of stunned. That is a sentence she's never heard me say before. But then: "I don't like the idea of you going to a strange party while I'm out of town."

"Mom," I say, "I'm seventeen years old. I can take perfectly good care of myself. And I wouldn't talk about strange parties if I were you. I mean…hello! Miss Hippie Happening, pass the brownies." I snap another photo. My mother hates when I do that during a conversation, let alone an argument. But I keep snapping and yapping, "I mean, really…you're always telling me to get out and associate with my peers. And here I am associating up a storm. Really, you don't have to worry."

"Okay. Fine. Go." She doesn't really mean it. She's just so frustrated with me. That's our little dance, my mother's and mine. Just keep saying the opposite of whatever the other person says even if it means contradicting yourself.

I cave. "I don't even want to go." That's the truth and my mom knows it.

"You should go out and have fun." The opposite game—expertly played.

"Okay, I'll go," I say. "But the chances of my having fun are precisely nonexistent." I snap another photo—this one of my mother's face. Mentally, I entitle it "Exasperation." I wonder if it will pass muster with Mr. Chappell.

"Will you please stop doing that?" she says. She makes a move to snatch the camera out of my hand.

If I were a more evolved human, I'd explain to her about the Incomplete and how it made my world shift on its axis. About how all my axes keep shifting. First, my so-called family and now my academic career. It's like my life is a riddle: how many axes does one person's world have? And how many ways can they go wacko? I wasn't enough to keep my parents together and now I'm not enough to get an "A" in my Arts elective of all pathetic things. But I am not that evolved a human. So instead, I snap another picture.

"No! I won't. I won't stop doing that. Actually, fine, I will 'cause I'm out of here." I grab my backpack and storm into the garage.

She follows me. "Where do you think you're going?"

I have no idea where I'm going. I just had this dramatic exit building up inside me. I just want out.

"I'm not driving you," Mom says. Low blow.

"I'll get there myself."

"Come on, Mari, don't be ridiculous. Where are you going?"

"To Daddy's." I know that makes no sense. He's busy this weekend. But it's a knee-jerk reaction. If my mother's going to play the driving card, I get to play the other parent card.

"You can't bike into the city," Mom says.

"Why not?"

"Mari…" Her tone softens a tad. "Daddy…" She doesn't want to say out loud that he doesn't want me. Not right now. Not this weekend. I wish she would. I wish she'd just say it.

"Fine! I'll just go…somewhere…else!"

I hop onto my bike and head out the garage, my camera still dangling around my neck. It thumps against my chest as I pedal.

"Okay, okay…I'll drive you!" my mom calls after. "Mari! It's going to rain!"

I pay no attention, just keep pedaling furiously down the driveway, skidding over the slick jacaranda carpet, pretending I know where I'm headed. At the end of the driveway, I turn onto the street and pedal hard into the curve.

A few moments later, Kelly's shiny black Jetta pulls up alongside me. Wouldn't you know I'd run into the girly-girls right now? Amanda sticks her head out the window. "Nice ride!"

The usual suspects are stuffed into the back seat. Vanessa says, "So correct of you. Like environmentally."

"That's me," I say, eyes on the road. "Save the planet." I flash a peace sign, choking on the Jetta's exhaust as they speed off.

Here comes the incline that always gets my thighs. I rise off the seat for extra push through this wooded stretch. Pedal, pedal, pedal. A raindrop splashes on my head, a coming attraction—ominous clouds are gathering quickly as though in time-lapse. Drizzle turns into full-blown rain as I reach the crest of the hill. At least I can coast for a while.

I let myself exhale as I hit a curve in the road… at the same moment a Jeep appears out of nowhere barreling toward me. I can see a young guy at the wheel, a guitar riding shotgun. As if in slo-mo, I watch the Jeep head for a pothole. He hits it straight on, sending the guitar flying in front of his face. The Jeep wobbles over the double line, way over the line, careening toward the shoulder of the road. And me. I swerve and hurtle into an embankment. A boulder rises toward me. I turn the handlebars hard. But too late and not hard enough. My front wheel smashes into the rock. The force propels me. I feel myself become airborne—over the handlebars, over the wheel, over the boulder…smack into a tree. Whomp!

I might be dying, especially if death welcomes you with the smell of honey and a lavender-blue aura. Oh-my-God, there really must be angels, because a silky veil—like wings—brushes my face. I flash on all the times I thought it would be so much easier to be dead, not that I ever remotely intended to do anything about it. Then I get it—no celestial fragrance, no lilac light, no friggin' wings. My head made contact with the trunk of a jacaranda; its lavender-blue flowers are raining down on me.

My hand flies to my skull. An instant goose egg. Wooziness washes over me, my visual cortex wheeling like a Spirograph. I close my eyes, but the colors keep swirling on the back of my eyelids like when you have a fever. Gradually, thankfully, they merge into the usual eyes-shut darkness. When I finally open them, I feel like my two eyes are not quite speaking to each other, like watching a 3D movie without the glasses.

I lie there—*like a slug*—that's the way I see myself, like the line from that movie *A Christmas Story*. I watch it every December, not without embarrassment, sometimes for forty-eight hours straight. It crosses my mind that *A Christmas Story* may be the last thing I ever think of before I die of head trauma. And this weird faraway sound may be the last thing I ever hear. I listen. Not so far away. It's coming from me. A deep yowl of a groan reverberating in my head. I tap my forehead gingerly. It's the kind of sore that's a little scary; the pain is bigger and deeper than expected and makes me suck in air so sharply I choke a little. It will take some effort to decide whether or not I can move. The sky opens up with a walloping clap of thunder as if it were a faucet and someone just removed the little water-conservation thingie.

I scooch myself onto all fours before I can even think about standing up. I stay there for a long moment, hands and knees under me, supporting me like the legs of a table. A very wobbly table. I rock back and forth—shifting weight from arms to legs, legs to arms—working up enough momentum to attempt to stand. A siren is coming to get me. But no, it's just the tinkle of the little bells dangling from this stupid blouse echoing in my skull. Thank God I didn't die in this relic of a top because I wouldn't be caught dead wearing the thing.

There, on all fours, I spot something off the road, deep in the trees. I squint through the rain. It's a VW van. Really old. I lift my hands from the ground, a primate giving standing erect a try, and make my way over. Its windows are shattered, three tires are missing, and the fourth is shredded to nothing. The driver's door hangs open on one hinge. Ivy has wrapped its way around the carcass. Through the driving rain, through the foliage, through the decades-thick crust of dirt, I make out the ghost of a psychedelic paint job. Swirls and paisleys and flowers and amoeba hallucinations. I stagger over and climb in.

CHAPTER
3

SUN STREAMS in through the windshield. The warmth feels good, but there's a cramp in my leg. I reach down to rub it away, but even that little bit of movement comes with a headache. There they are— the twin bumps on my head. A double-header—I'd crack myself up if I had the energy. I touch them lightly. Big time swellings...ovoid and hard...from my hairline halfway down onto my forehead. My eyes flutter open. Where am I anyway? Then I remember. The rain and the Jeep and the tree.

It must be morning because the sun is coming up. My mom must be freaking out. I wonder if she called my dad, in which case they both must be freaking out. And Sarah's probably joined in on the whole freak-out by now. I'm not going to lie—there's an awful, miserable, nasty corner of my brain that doesn't mind if everyone's thinking about me. I don't want them to be sick with worry, but a little concern directed my way—there's something horribly satisfying there. Not proud of myself for that.

The truth is I am probably still asleep anyway. This must be one of those moments when you think you're waking up from a dream, only to have it keep going. Sometimes it takes a series of waking-ups (wakings-up?) before you accomplish the real thing. I've had those dreams where you're acutely aware of that whole phenomenon. Infinite REM regress. But this is a doozey, and accompanied, no less, by distant dream music—a tambourine and a flute. No, not a flute. A recorder like we learned to play in elementary school. I close my eyes tight, then open them. Close. Open. Maybe I can blink away this aural hallucination. No. The music is moving closer. Like a driver stopping short whose arm snaps out to restrain a child in the passenger seat, my hand flies instinctively to my camera. Still there, hanging around my neck. Miraculously, it seems to have survived intact. I stand slowly, afraid of setting off any bodily alarms, and make my way out of the van. I have to squint against the sun.

From the distance, two figures dance toward me along an overgrown trail. A boy in ratty jeans and a tie-dyed shirt, his hair stringy to his shoulders. A girl in a long dress made of Indian bedspread fabric—the kind they sell at the Hare Krishna center in the city. The dress pulls taut against her pregnant belly. The guy blows into the recorder while the girl beats the tambourine against her hip. Quite the mirage. Okay... ready to wake up now. I take a step in their direction, expecting them to vanish back into my imagination. Instead they just keep skipping closer.

I glance over my shoulder. The bus is still there. Seems real, but that's impossible. I turn my head back too fast. Woozy. Very. That Spirograph starts tracing roulette wheels in my brain again, corkscrewing around, only this time my eyes are open. I sink to the ground.

The boy and girl rush to my side. "What happened?" he asks.

"You okay?" The girl rests a hand on my shoulder. Her wavy light brown hair widens like a pyramid, turning golden at the ends. The smattering of freckles across the bridge of her nose makes her seem like a little girl, even though she's super pregnant.

"I guess I had a little accident," I say.

The girl pulls a bandana out of her macramé bag and dabs at a trail of dried blood on my cheek. I push her hand away and try to stand.

"Hang on," the girl says like she's talking to a child. She keeps her hand on my shoulder. "Take it easy." She stuffs the bandana back in her bag and pulls out a bag of trail mix, starts munching the nuts and raisins. She offers me some, but I shake my head no.

"I'm okay. Really," I insist. "Just help me find my bike so I can get out of here."

The guy picks up the twisted wreck that was my bicycle. It's almost too painful to look at. It looks a lot like my life.

"You're not okay," he says. "Where were you headed?"

"Into the city."

"Far out!" the girl chimes in. "You can come with us."

I shake my head. No chance.

"We're headin' for the Haight," he says.

"That's where it's all happenin'," she adds.

"Oh...kay...," I say. Have I heard of any mental patients escaping recently?

"Sam's in a band," the girl offers. "He's Sam. I'm Jennifer." He places one arm around what she has left of a waist and nuzzles her hair aside, burying his face in her neck.

I figure the band must be some sort of retro hippie-chic thing, but I'm not about to interview them about it.

"You have to come with us!" Jennifer exclaims. "It's going to be so groovy!"

"No, really," I say, "I'll just call my dad to come get me." I rummage in my backpack for my phone and wait for it to spark to life. Nothing.

"Whoa!" Sam's eyes pop out of his head like a cartoon. "Dig it," he says. "Is that a Star Trek thing? Like a communicator or something?"

"It's just my phone. It's not due out for a couple of weeks, but my dad's in tech, and he's always giving me stuff to compensate for his lack of attention and his general type-A personality, not to mention the whole abandonment issue."

"Does he work for the government?" Sam asks. "Like NASA or the CIA?"

"Sometimes, I guess. He works for Digitech. He designs software."

Jennifer rubs her belly in concentric circles. "Like pillows?"

I laugh, but it comes out like a snort. Which is all that joke deserves. "He designed the GUI on this model."

"The gooey?" asks Jennifer.

"They say people are going to line up for days when it's released," I explain. I offer the phone to Sam to have a look, but he holds up his hands, palms forward like it's radioactive—no thanks.

"No, man," he says. "That's got to be classified. You know, they get you if you know more than you're supposed to know, you know? 'Nuff said." He steps back as I call my dad. Or try to anyway. Shit. No signal.

≈୰≈

A VW van rounds the bend in the road as we emerge from the thicket, Sam and Jennifer sandwiching me between them. The van is nearly new, robin's egg blue. Sam waves wildly as it approaches. "Here comes Jimmy!"

I'm not paying much attention, just tapping my phone like crazy, trying to get some bars. I don't remember this being a dead stretch before. Must have been the rain. Something must have blown. I wonder if either of these characters would let me use their phone. Before I can ask, the van pulls over. The driver slides open the passenger door. He is also working the long hair thing, but sort of mid-Beatle, not down his back. (The Beatles loom large in my dad's legend, so I'm embarrassingly familiar with their various phases, both musical and hair.)

"Hey, you freaks!" he calls to Sam and Jennifer. "Who's the kid?"

"She had a bad scene with a bike and a tree," says Sam.

"Bummer."

"She's coming with us to the city," says Jennifer. She nudges me closer to the van. But I'm fairly well planted.

"No. Really," I say. "It's a very generous offer, but my mother always told me never to get into strange cars with strange people. Not that I'm using 'strange' in any pejorative way, more in the unknown, alien kind of way…not that I'm saying you bear any resemblance to actual aliens…Anyway, have fun." I go back to tapping my index finger on my phone. Nothing. I try the fallback: turn it off, then back on. More nothing.

Jennifer throws her arms around me. "We can't just leave you here."

Sam leans into the van, "We can't just leave her here, Jimmy."

"Fine, fine," Jimmy says. "Just get her in and let's hit the road. The guys are waiting."

"No," I say firmly. "I'm not going with you."

This Jimmy guy shrugs, throws the van into gear. Sam hops in, grabs Jennifer's hand and hoists her up.

She settles onto the seat next to him and offers me a quick wave before Sam slides the door shut and the van pulls away.

That was one close encounter of the weirdness kind.

I glance back to the thicket of trees and spot my mangled bike. Then I stare at the long stretch of road ahead. The van is nearly rounding the bend. A decal is plastered to its rear window. Some sort of symbol—a Mandala, I think—shimmers in the sunlight. Before I can think about it: "Wait!" I shout. "Wait!" I take off after, flailing my arms over my head.

The van screeches to a halt, slams into reverse. As it backs up, I realize it's got one of those funky old California license plates, the kind the hipsters think are so cool—black with gold lettering. The van screeches to a stop in front of me. Sam leans forward to throw open the door.

"I guess I'll come," I say. "Just for the ride."

"What else did you have in mind?" Jimmy asks, flashing what he obviously thinks is a killer smile. Actually it *is* a killer smile, but he doesn't have to know it. Obnoxious.

I'd prefer minding my own business in the rear of the van, but Sam and Jennifer are making out back there. (I mean, give it a rest.) So I climb into the passenger seat. I dig for the seatbelt, but it is stuck out of reach. I shove my hand deep into the creases of the seat.

"I can't find the seatbelt."

"What?" says Jimmy.

"The seatbelt," I say. "It's stuck."

"Don't have one."

He could just admit it's broken, but whatever. Guys and their vehicles.

The inside of the van is decked out more like a den than a car—no, more like a guy's stinky dorm room, though, goes without saying, my knowledge of same is entirely cinematic, the olfactory factor so often referenced, as in: "Take out the trash, dude." A dank musk sticks to the interior, sort of sickly sweet, sort of sour. Some food stuff has gone bad somewhere in here—an avocado or a banana. I crack the window.

Batik fabric covers the back windows. A couple of guitars lie on the empty seats. Several drum cases are crammed in the way back. A crystal prism dangles from the rearview mirror, catching the sunlight. This Jimmy guy taps it, casting rainbows across the dashboard and across his face. His eyes are already a color I've never seen before—like the bottom of the ocean, dark gray-green and flecked with gold. It's hard not to stare at them.

"Somewhere over the rainbow," he sings. It's almost like he expects me to sing along, and I feel my face go hot, so hot I know my cheeks must be pink, practically glowing. I roll my eyes to let him know I will not be participating in this sing-along and that

I don't think he's cute or anything, no matter what color my cheeks happen to be. Or his eyes.

His brown corduroy pants are worn at the knee, and his long-sleeved Henley T-shirt is misbuttoned. I have an impulse to correct the buttoning, but no way. His hair, super thick, flips at the base of his neck and does a swoop thing over his right eye. You can tell his hair does that naturally, not as the result of his spending major mirror time, which in my never-to-be-humble opinion is downright repugnant in guys.

"I'm Jimmy," he says.

I don't know whether to tell him I heard Sam say his name, which would imply I was paying attention, or whether to pretend his name is news to me. I feel doomed either way. I just nod. It feels weird not to spit out something pithy, feels like something inside me got stuck. Good practice, though. Silence is a response option I've been meaning to acquire. No time like the present.

"And you?" he asks. "Do you have a name?"

"Mari. Mari Caldwell. Tamara actually. That's what Mari's short for. Tamara." Unstuck. Clearly. "Tamara Caldwell. Stupid name. In elementary school, the kids would always say, See you tomorrow, Tamara. So I started going with the whole Mari thing."

"Nice to meet you, Mari Tamara Caldwell."

I'm not sure if he's making fun of me. I wouldn't blame him. What's my problem anyway? It's either all or nothing when it comes to the relationship between my mouth and words. Why couldn't I just say my name like a normal human? And why do I care what this guy thinks of me? Some freak driving an old VW van.

He taps the prism again. "*Someday I'll wish upon a star…And wake up where the clouds are far behind me…*" He calls back to Sam, "I've got it! A name for the band. Crystal Prism!"

"I like it," says Sam. "It's got a certain…"

"Destined for obscurity quality," I say. Because there's no getting around it, it's a horrible name.

"You don't like it?" Jimmy asks.

"I guess it works in a New Age, have-a-nice-day, let's find our third eye sort of way. But haven't we been there, done that?

Jimmy eyeballs me, confused. I get it—sometimes I don't compute.

"Now that's a name," says Sam. "Been There, Done That."

"If you're looking for your garden variety, hackneyed, reverse commentary on adolescent angst and rejection of the status quo."

"You've got to love the way this girl talks," Jimmy says. And then he smiles again. A smile so natural, so relaxed, so unselfconscious and easy. The exact opposite of everything…me.

Nobody says anything for a few minutes, and then Sam pipes up. "What if we call ourselves More? So that every time a concert is announced and they say so-and-so's going to be there and so-and-so's going to be there…and more…everyone will think it's us?"

CHAPTER
4

WE'RE CRUISING through Tiburon, looping down toward the ferry landing, when Jimmy pulls into a gas station. It's kind of funky, with these narrow pumps that remind me of Coke machines in old movies, only in Big Bird yellow. They're marked Regular and Unleaded—as though they were selling coffee or something. A guy in some kind of uniform dashes over to the van and starts spritzing the windshield. He doesn't seem like your average stoplight homeless guy with a flimsy squeegee and a spray bottle full of dirty suds. Jimmy waves him away—no time—and honks the horn. A guy slides out from under an old Mustang, wipes his hands on a rag, and peels out of a pair of greasy overalls. Underneath, he's wearing faded jeans, more holes than denim. No doubt, Kelly and her posse could identify the designer from the Rorschach rips. I wonder how this guy could have afforded them on a grease monkey's salary.

The guy dashes over to the van, waving good-bye to the station owner who doesn't seem to care all that much that his employee is taking off. The guy bounds into the van and off we go.

"This is Mari-Tamara-Caldwell," says Jimmy.

"Pablo Jose Rodriguez. P.J.," says the guy. He seems a little older than the others—wavy black hair and olive skin. He launches right into some patter.

"There's this explorer flying over the Himalayas, see? And this big storm comes up and his plane crashes. He's lost for weeks. Living on nothing but snow. He's close to death, crawling along on his hands and knees when, suddenly, his head bumps into something. He looks up and sees this big neon sign. Himalaya Restaurant. Specialty of the house…Shlemma Pie."

"Hold it there, man," says Jimmy, as he veers over to pick up another guy standing in front of a shabby apartment building. Bamboo lettering over the door declares the place "Shangri-La." A couple of tiki torches stand guard.

"Boo-Boo!" shouts Jimmy.

Boo-Boo wedges himself into the back of the van. He waves to me as though we already know each other, and I see that his fingertips are wrapped in Band-Aids.

"Boo-Boo's our drummer," says Jimmy as he pulls back onto the road "Meet Mari-Tamara-Caldwell." If it were anyone else, I'd tell him to shut-the-fuck up. But I just keep my mouth shut. After all, he's really making an effort to do the polite introduction thing so you've got to give him points for etiquette.

Boo-Boo wears overalls with no shirt underneath—striped train engineer overalls. He immediately starts pounding out a beat on the side of a drum case, his wire rim glasses bobbing on his nose. P. J. fiddles on his bass. As for Sam, he's lip-locked with Jennifer, but manages a thumbs-up as the guys find some sort of groove, I'd guess they'd call it.

Frankly, I don't know what they'd call anything. They're not like anybody I've ever met before. They're all a little older than me, maybe nineteen or twenty, but they must have gone to another school. Actually, they don't really seem like Kentfield types. I'm betting they went to Tamalpais High. A guy in my class transferred from there, and he had the same leftover hippie freak kind of vibe.

We ride along like that for a while, the guys in the back pounding and strumming, Jimmy driving and smiling to himself every now and then like a really good idea has just dawned on him. Before long, we crest over a hill. And there it is—the Golden Gate Bridge and, beyond, the city of San Francisco.

"Feast your eyes, my friends," says Jimmy. "The land of Oz."

Whoops and cheers bounce off the back of the van. I'll say one thing: these guys are not lacking for enthusiasm. Compared to all the uber-cool hipster types that seem to be around lately, they're...I'm not exactly sure what they are...but they are most definitively not uber-cool hipster types.

Jimmy flips on the radio. The Monkees sing in all their bubble gum merriment. *"Then I saw her face… Now I'm a believer…Not a trace of doubt in my mind…"*

Jimmy snickers. "If this manufactured Muzak can make it, we can make it."

"Who'd ever have thought their lunch boxes would be worth a fortune?" I ask.

"They are?" asks P.J., incredulous.

"You know," I say, "like on eBay."

"Over on the east bay?" Boo-Boo asks.

"EBay," I say, pronouncing it as though I'm speaking to a foreigner. "Like the web site."

Sam nods conspiratorially. "It's a government thing, isn't it?"

"Probably," I agree. "Aren't they all?"

"'Nuff said," says Sam, sotto voce.

These guys are pretty plugged in. Most of the kids in my school never give the big governmental picture a thought.

The bridge is upon us. An instant later, we're upon it. My breath starts to get a little jagged and, even worse, stops being automatic. Poundy heart is going to come next. The more I try to talk myself off the ledge of the impending thump-thump, thump-thump, the harder my heart pounds. By the time we reach the bridge, it's doing old Edgar Allan Poe proud. I bury my head in my hands. But that doesn't do the trick. I lower my head between my knees—

embarrassing, but less embarrassing than passing out, which is a distinct possibility.

"Are you going to be sick?" Jimmy asks.

I shake my head no, whacking it knee to knee.

"Please don't throw up."

"I'll be okay," I say, raising my head a few inches to offer Jimmy a wan sidelong smile. Not very convincing. "I have a slight case of gephyrophobia. Actually, I refuse to call it a full-out phobia. It's really just a manifestation of my neuroses, which admittedly are numerous, but there's no such thing as gephyroneurosis, so if I'm going to go ahead and label it, I've got to go with the whole phobia thing."

Jimmy glances at me: "huh?"

"Bridges," I say. "I have a fear of bridges." Which, truthfully, is a major impediment if you live in Marin. A certifiable handicap.

"Even the Golden Gate?"

"Actually, if you must know, ten men were killed building this bridge."

"Building. Not crossing."

"A minor detail," I say, dropping my head deeper between my knees.

"You're missing the view," Jimmy says. "It's spectacular."

"I'm sure it's breathtaking, but given the fact that I'm having a bit of difficulty breathing already, I'll pass."

"Come on," Jimmy persuades. He reaches over and places his hand on top of mine where it is resting on my thigh. "This could be the place where all your dreams come true."

"More like nightmares," I say. "Actually, I have this dream all the time. It doesn't end well."

Jimmy doesn't say anything else, but keeps hold of my hand. I can't believe how much that calms me; that's the only reason I let him keep his hand there. The feel of his hand on top of mine—I could ride all the way to Mexico like that. I mean, if I had to.

The Monkees finish singing, and Jimmy takes his hand away. I figure that means we're across the bridge. I look up tentatively and breathe again, finally. I've made it into the city.

Something about the skyline looks different, but I can't put my finger on it. Something feels missing. Something tall. The Hyatt Regency maybe. Or is it the Transamerica Pyramid? Actually, it's both of them. How had I not heard about either one of those buildings biting the dust? Why are they always knocking down perfectly good buildings? I guess my mom has a point about my never picking up a newspaper or even watching the news on TV.

"There's a runaway shelter down in the Haight," Jimmy says. "We've got to make one stop, then I'll take you there."

"I'm not a runaway, thank you very much," I declare rather high-handedly. "My dad will come get me." Jimmy stops at a red light, and I make a move to get out of the van.

"I'm not letting you out here," he says. "We'll make our stop and then I'll take you right to your dad's. I promise."

We are in the middle of the financial district at ten o'clock in the morning, just when things should be buzzing, but there doesn't seem to be the typical crush of business suits. Some, of course, but not the usual thick of it. Is today a bank holiday? That might make my dad hard to find.

"Okay," I say, "if you promise." For some reason, I believe that this Jimmy guy is someone who keeps his promises, even though my history with the human race has given me little cause to believe that about too many people.

"So," says Jimmy, "you don't like any of the names for our band that you've heard so far. Let's hear you come up with something."

"Me?" I ask.

"You," he dares me.

My mind goes strangely blank. A pop quiz I wasn't prepared for.

"We need a name that takes a stand," says Sam.

"The Easel?" says P.J. I let out a weird little laugh; it comes out more like a snort.

"Maybe there's a creature as yet unexploited," offers P.J. "Crickets, Beatles, Monkees...Let's think animal kingdom."

"We need an animal with rhythm," says Boo-Boo.

"Spoken like a true drummer," Jimmy says.

"We could google animals with rhythm," I say. I'm trying to redeem myself for not being able to come up with something. And for the snort.

"Google?" says Jimmy. It seems like he might be considering that as the name, so I go along with the idea. As band names go, it's utterly lame, of course, but I have heard worse. Of course, they'd be opening themselves up for a world of legal woes.

"Google's not bad," I say.

"What part of the world does the google come from?" asks Boo-Boo.

I snort again—pretty funny—and play along. "Oh, you know, the craggy mountainous terrain that abuts the Eastern portion of the Indian Ocean."

"Dig it," says P.J.

"It's an area known for its biologic diversity, kind of like the Galapagos," I continue, "and the google is just one of the many flat-billed amphibious creatures that populate the region."

"Wow!" says Boo-Boo, "the google. Never heard of it. Where does it fall on the food chain?" These guys are really good at playing a riff—as good as Sarah.

Sam breaks his lip-lock with Jennifer. "We shouldn't rush into anything. This is going to be the name that's going to stick with us for…I don't know… three or four years."

"Think big, my friend," says Jimmy. "This is going to be the name that's engraved on our gold records." He's not one bit full of himself when he says this, just excited by the idea, like a little kid. I always thought it was stupid when people said enthusiasm was contagious, but all of a sudden when I glance over at Jimmy, I feel like something deep in my chest has been plugged into an electrical socket and someone just flipped the switch. It's a little disconcerting, but also a little addictive, like I'm poised, waiting for the next jolt.

We wind our way up from the water. Throngs of kids—duded up for some sort of throwback festival, there's always one of those these days—mill around the corner of Haight and Ashbury.

"I thought there was a Gap here," I consider, as Jimmy cruises through the intersection.

"Oh no," he says, completely deadpan. "The streets have always come together right there."

He's quick, this Jimmy. Maybe I should introduce him to Sarah.

We drive a little more, heading up Geary to where it crosses Fillmore. The auditorium is on the corner. Remarkably, there's a parking space just a few doors down and Jimmy pulls right in. Whenever I come to this neighborhood with my dad, we circle and circle until, half the time, we just give up and decide to go somewhere else where, frankly, the parking isn't much better, but at least there are structures where you can fork over the big bucks for the privilege of leaving your car somewhere while you get something to eat.

The guys tumble out of the van into the Fillmore. A sign above the ticket window reads: "Once Inside—

No Outsy-Insy." I trail behind as they climb to the second floor. A copper bucket at the top of the stairs is filled with apples. Jimmy grabs one and chomps a bite, then tosses another to me.

Once, about a year and a half ago, Sarah and I went to see the Black Crowes at the Fillmore. It was kind of a big deal. Our parents had to have this whole pow-wow about whether or not we should be allowed to be dropped off and enter the premises on our own, but they finally decided that since we were veritable paragons of maturity, we could go. My dad drove us and spent the entire ride regaling us with the history of the place. Yack-yack-yack. We'd heard of it, of course, and knew that it was *the* place back in the so-called day, but he acted like we were making a sacred pilgrimage. Turned out that the show—like so much of life—was more exciting to plan for than to see. But I remember thinking that the ultra-violet lights in the chandeliers were super cool.

Today, in the light of day, it's just a cavernous room. A card table is set up at the far end for sign-ups. A line of guys, a few girls maybe, mill around in front of it.

The guys from the van scatter and suddenly I wonder what I'm doing here. Risk-taking is anathema to me. I decide I'm going to ditch these weirdos, not that they'd even notice, and try my dad again.

Still nothing. Zero bars. And the same little red "X" that keeps popping up when I try texting. What's up with this piece-of-shit phone? So much for cutting edge. Thanks for nothing, Steve Jobs. I consider asking to use someone else's phone, but no one has theirs out at the moment, which is pretty weird.

I take the Leica out of my backpack, hold it up to my eye and scan the room. Jennifer and Sam are wrapped around each other, swaying to music only they can hear. It's quite a sight, what with her massive belly and all. Her eyes are half closed, and she looks like a little kid fighting sleep. For the first time, I realize she's probably not that much older than I am. Maybe just a year or two, if that. I'd be scared shitless to be having a baby, but she seems to be rocking an otherworldly sort of serenity. Beatific, you might say. Downright Madonna like. As in your traditional Madonna, not the let's-reinvent-ourselves-one-more-time-for-lack-of-authentic-innovation Madonna. I snap a photo of Sam and Jennifer. Click.

In a far corner of the room, Boo-Boo is a blur of air drumming. Click.

P.J. holds court with a bunch of guys hanging out near the sign-in desk. Click.

And then there's Jimmy. He stands alone on the deserted stage, eyes closed tight, soaking up the vibe of the room like he's trying to absorb the history of the place through his pores. I lower the camera from my eye and just look at him.

P.J. leaps up on stage, waves a flyer in Jimmy's face. He studies the paper then jumps down and crosses the ballroom to the makeshift sign-up desk. I edge close enough to hear.

"We want to sign up," he says.

"Name?" asks the girl behind the card table.

"Jimmy Westwood."

"Of the band," she corrects him.

"We're not sure yet."

"Can't sign you up without a name."

"Tell you what," says Jimmy. "For now just call us the Band With No Name."

"Got one of those." She reads from her list. "Band With No Name, The No Names, The Nameless Four…"

Jimmy holds up a hand to stop her. "Okay, Okay," he says, "we'll come up with something." He beckons the guys to his side.

"It's bad karma to rush into anything," warns P.J.

Sam agrees. "We shouldn't cave to pressure from external forces, man."

Boo-Boo chimes in. "Yeah, remember, like you said, this could be our name for, like, all of history."

"Or at least a couple months," says P.J.

Jimmy looks from his bandmates to the girl seated on the dented aluminum folding chair at the card table. She is filling in the cracks in her vinyl boots with a black magic marker, though who cares, since the main purpose of the boots is to draw attention to the vast gulf between where they stop and her miniskirt begins.

"We'll be back," says Jimmy, then he turns away from the girl at the table. He might be looking for me. Probably not. Just in case, I don't want him to catch me staring at him, so I raise my camera to my eye and start snapping. I back up a few steps to get a wider angle. True to the klutz I am, I bump into someone. More like slam. My backpack basically throws up all over the place.

"Hey, watch out!"

"I'm sorry," I say. I whip around to find this guy who is some sort of force of nature. Whoa. Like all these other freaks, he's got the long hair, but his is tied back with a leather cord, black like his skin-tight leather pants. Jimmy is tall and lean, sort of fluid in the way he moves, but this guy is solid, muscle, all earth. Not that I even know why I'm comparing them. He stoops to help me gather my stuff.

"I'm sorry I didn't see you," I say. "Of course, lacking eyes in the back of my head, that would have been impossible, it goes without saying. But I guess I'm saying it anyway. Redundancy R Us."

"Don't sweat it, Sunshine," he says. His voice is low, hoarse, almost a growl. He nods toward my camera, lifting his chin in its direction, his jaw sharp, hard-angled. "You here to take some pics?"

"Yeah. I mean no. It's just, you know, something to look good on my applications. College time and all that." I swirl my up-pointed index finger in a corkscrew through the air: whoopee! "Actually, I have to take a picture of a person. A portrait. To wipe out an Incomplete. It's complicated."

"I'm a person."

"I can see that," I say.

"You could swing by my place and take a few shots."

"That's a very generous offer," I say, "but I'm with this band. I mean, I'm here with a band. That is to say, I'm not actually affiliated with a band. I'm not a musician or anything. God knows musicality is not one of my strong suits. I mean, as gifts go, if musicality were one, mine would never have been wrapped. In fact, the box would be empty. I just happened to come with them, the band guys. I mean, they're just giving me a ride. Those guys..." I wave my hand in the direction of Jimmy and the others. They're in a huddle—trying to come up with a name, I'm guessing.

"Well, well, well...If it isn't my old pal, Jimmy Westwood," says Leather Pants. He crosses to them and insinuates himself into their circle.

"Hey!" Jimmy exclaims. "What are you doing here?"

"Same as you. Signing up for the big showdown." Leather Pants mimes drawing six-guns.

"So where's the rest of your crew?" Jimmy asks.

"I've gone solo."

Jimmy nods. "So, Al...," he says.

Leather Pants cuts him off. "Name's Royce."

"Not to me it isn't," says Jimmy, shaking his head. "Rodney Aloysius Roystoski," Jimmy announces. This Royce guy glares. "That's what you'll always be to me."

Jennifer leans close to my ear and whispers, "They've got history. They used to write songs together."

"What happened?" I ask.

"Nina happened," says Jennifer, like I should know what that means. "Classic," she adds.

On cue, Royce asks Jimmy, "How's Nina?"

Jennifer cocks her head toward the two guys—*see what I mean?*

"She's good," answers Jimmy.

"You know why they're doing the whole original song thing, don't you?" Royce asks. "Record company's going to be here. Winner bags a contract."

Sam nods knowingly. "Corporate America rears its ugly head."

Royce laughs like someone who can already feel the pen in his hand. Then he flashes a smile—directed right at me—throws in a half-wink and heads across the ballroom.

"He thinks he's such a rebel," says Sam disdainfully.

"Yeah," says Jimmy. "A rebel without a clue." He watches this Royce guy saunter over to a couple of girls swinging their legs off the edge of the stage.

"That guy's a walking downer," says Jimmy.

"Forget about him," advises P.J.

"Let's get out of here," Jimmy says. "We've got a few days. We'll come back when we've got a name. A fan-fuckin'-tastic name."

CHAPTER
5

THE VAN cruises past deserted warehouses and vacant lots. Weird. "Are you sure you're on Bryant?" I wonder aloud.

Jimmy points at a street sign. Bryant.

"Are you sure you have the right address?" he asks.

"Of course I am."

"Well," says Jimmy, "this is it."

A chain-link fence surrounds a massive hole in the ground. An address is scrawled in paint on a board nailed to the fence. It's my father's address. "This is crazy," I say. "I've been here a thousand times."

"It's a government thing," says Sam. "They've beamed him up."

"Just let me out here," I say, gathering my backpack.

"I don't feel good about this," says Jimmy. But what does he know? He's just a random guy in a van, smile notwithstanding. He's right, of course. I don't feel good about this either. Something strange has happened to the neighborhood. When my dad moved in, he gave me a whole song and dance about how hip the area was, even though it seemed to me that his version of hip meant a building full of divorced men trying to be cool with such a vengeance that they were likely to pull a muscle. It doesn't look so hip today by anyone's standards. It's borderline creepy. No matter what this handmade sign says, I must be on the wrong block.

Even so, I jump out of the van and wave. "Thanks for the ride."

I watch the van pull away and, I'm not going to lie, it feels a little like I'm losing something—not sure what—but a chance at something. I pull out my apparently bug-riddled phone and call my father. Nothing. Has there been some sort of meteor shower? Sun spots? The heart of the city can't be a dead zone. Stupid satellite. Isn't modern technology supposed to account for things going wrong? I mean, really, what's the point otherwise?

I spot an old phone booth half a block away. That's what I'm talking about, the whole self-consciously hip thing. The homeowner's association must have thought it would be cool to preserve a vintage phone booth, give the area charm. The door accordions to one side, and I step in. This thing is no TARDIS from *Dr. Who*. It's cramped and reeks of cigarettes and urine. I hold my breath against the stench. They haven't even bothered to convert the phone yet—no touch screen. Taking the retro bit a little far, don't you think? I fish in my backpack for some loose coins, slide a quarter into the slot. Before I can dial, a woman's voice speaks to me. "You have fifteen cents credit," she says.

"I beg your pardon."

"You deposited twenty-five cents," she says. "You have fifteen cents credit." It seems like she's a real person or else robo-voices have really taken a leap.

"If you say so," I say, and then, since she is a real person, I ask her to try my dad's number for me since my general phone mojo seems to have gone so haywire.

"My pleasure," says the voice. Definitely a real person. What a crazy job: dialing phone numbers for strangers. I hear the tick–tick-tick of something mechanical, then the voice comes back on. "I'm very sorry, but that number appears to have been disconnected."

"That's not possible."

"I'm very sorry."

I hang up the phone and step out of the booth. A little swell of panic is rising in me; I need to figure out what's going on. I don't think of myself as being directionally challenged, and an address is an address…Maybe there are two Bryants. Maybe it's a North versus South thing. Or Avenue versus Place. Maybe this one's in a whole other part of town. That must be it, because it's fairly quiet in my dad's neighborhood and this place is really noisy. Down the block, people are shouting. In fact, the shouting is getting closer and closer.

A horde of people is moving down the street like a tidal wave, carrying signs, no less. "Make love, not war!" "Stop the war, I wanna get off!" "War is not healthy for children and other living things!" And chanting. Like lunatics. "Hey, hey, LBJ, how many kids did you kill today?"

Now I get it. They must be making a movie. I look around for the camera, but can't spot it. Probably some indie production being shot on a Hi-Def hand-held the size of a credit card.

The marchers swarm around me, giving me a major case of claustrophobia. I try to elbow my way out of the mob, but find myself trapped in a web of arms shooting skyward, flashing peace signs. I ride the wave to the edge of the crowd until I manage to jostle myself closer to the shelter of the buildings, hoping to duck into a store, when something sharp stabs my hipbone. It's the metal frame of a newsstand. My eyes fall on the headline: VIETNAM WAR ESCALATES. For a two-bit production with no visible camera or lighting, they're being real sticklers for detail. The date on the newspaper even reads June 17, 1967.

I stare at the date for a minute. Then at the protesters. Then at the date. The guy manning the stand is playing the radio—a transistor radio. A voice bellows from the bright orange box. "Hey, teens, school's out! And this is going to be one super groovy summer. A summer of peace, a summer of music, a summer of love! And now, with the number one song in the nation, here's the Strawberry Alarm Clock."

"Incense and Peppermints." What the…?

My fingers fly to the Siamese twin bumps on my skull. This is some dream. Or hallucination. Complete with props. I pick up the newspaper. There's something about a war in Israel. Okay, that makes sense. And something about the People's Republic of China testing its first hydrogen bomb. Not sure about that one. Thurgood Marshall was just nominated to the United States Supreme Court. Wasn't he the first African-American justice? I'm pretty sure he was. I remember that from AP US History. And wasn't that ages ago? Like in the sixties? At the bottom of the page, there's a little article about the Monterey Pop Festival. Jimi Hendrix set to play…tomorrow. That much history I know for sure, AP or no AP. Jimi Hendrix isn't playing anywhere tomorrow.

Unless it really is 1967.

"It's 1967?" I say to the news vendor. My voice sounds funny, constricted, like it knows I'm going to cry before I do.

"That's right," he says.

"1967? Like 19…67."

"You want the paper or not?" he asks.

I study the paper like it's got cooties. Ancient, fossilized cooties. How could I not have figured this out sooner? There must be something seriously wrong with me to take this long to get it. Of course, a regular human, even a quasi-regular human like myself, wouldn't expect to wake up one morning and find herself plunked down in another time. But still, I should have put it all together. There were so many signs. Signs pointed to the sixties everywhere I turned. The van. The guys. The hair…so much hair everywhere. And this street…no one's shooting a movie. This is real life. As real as life can be with zero bars on your phone. As real as life can be that's been over for decades. As real as life can be from before you were born. Way before.

Suddenly, everything seems hyper-real, like an old Technicolor movie and simultaneously surreal like a dream. That makes sense since this must be one of those dreams that feel uber real even when one part of your brain calmly—dare I say, cerebrally—articulates that it's just a dream while the other part maniacally yells, "This is no dream!" It's one of those. On steroids. One of those dreams where all you want to do is get home.

"That paper's going to cost you a dime," says the vendor.

I drop the paper onto the counter, shaking, and turn to face…the past.

For lack of any better plan, I hail a passing taxi and get in.

"Where to?" asks the driver.

"I'm not sure," I say. "Just out of here."

"I know where you want to go. Where all the kids want to go."

CHAPTER
6

I PEER outside the window of the back seat of the cab, searching for I'm not sure what. Whatever it is, it's not there. Nothing familiar. This is supposed to be an upscale area, a mix of new high-rises and old warehouses—the cool tech hub of the city. Gentrified, my mom would say in one of her flyers. Instead, today, it's a crummy mish-mosh. There's a mom and pop grocery store next door to a shop advertising Zig-Zag rolling papers and patchouli. An old coffee house, not Peet's or Starbucks, looks like the beatnik place where Audrey Hepburn went to philosophize with deep thinkers in one of those old movies I watched with my dad—*Funny Face*. The kind of place where people used to smoke and listen to finger-snap poetry and drink muddy espresso. I guess the times haven't a-changed there yet.

And there are so many people—all young—wandering the streets, more carnival than business district. Beads and feathers, jeans and fringe, tie-dye and daisy chains, bare feet and moccasins. Shirtless guys and girls swagged in velvet. Here, an American flag cape billows down the street. There, a cargo jacket is plastered with buttons like the ones that fell out of my mom's scrapbook. "God is a teeny bopper." "Reality is a crutch." "Who cares?" On one side of the street, a cardboard sign dangles around a guy's neck: ECO-MAN. On the other, a girl straddled atop a guy's shoulders undulates to the music coming from…everywhere. Part parade, part festival, part bazaar. All bonkers.

The cabdriver pulls over to the curb. "Here it is," he says.

"Here what is?"

He points to the street signs marking the intersection. Haight and Ashbury. I pay the driver and step out of the cab. A guy with a tangle of hair and a beard that looks like pubic hair is hawking a newspaper, *The Berkeley Barb*. Another, *The Oracle*. The scent of jasmine, I think, wafts through the air as he waves his papers. A couple of biker guys—Hells Angels?—all tricked out in leather, lounge on their bikes with square-toed boots propped against the handlebars. A girl skips down the street, dangling strings of beads from her arms, waving them at passersby. She drapes a strand over the head of a guy sitting in the middle of the sidewalk, legs stretched out in front of him. He has the gaunt, half-mast look of someone in need of a sandwich.

This can't be happening, I panic. *This can't be happening.* But it sure feels like it is. I need one of those objects to test myself—like in that Leo DiCaprio movie about dreams—something to test reality. But I can't come up with any such totem. I've gone through the looking glass and the universe on the other side is pretty convincing.

I stand there, stuck to the spot where the taxi deposited me. A girl thrusts a flower in my face. "No thanks," I say, "I didn't take my antihistamine today." I head down the block and pass a guy in full army regalia expounding to no one in particular. "Burn your draft card! Fight the establishment! Refuse to join the military industrial complex!" For real.

The sound of a man's voice over a loudspeaker blasts from a tour bus. It's a Grey Line with massive oval windows, most slid to the side so that the occupants can gawk more freely. The driver delivers his spiel, "Ladies and gentlemen, we're about to begin the only foreign tour in the continental United States." A bunch more windows slide open and the tourists crane their necks. One woman raises a doughy hand to shield the eyes of her daughter, a little girl wearing a hot pink headband. The girl smiles anyway, the sun flashing off her braces. The bus cruises on. "Here in the Haight-Ashbury neighborhood," says the driver, "you will find the hippie in their natural habitat..." *He got that right*, I think, *this is a friggin' zoo.*

A grimy palm appears. "Spare change?"

I pick up my pace, but he persists. "I'm a poet," he says. "Support the arts?"

"I watch PBS," I say, "leave me alone."

I'm running now, before I even realize it, through this sidewalk tilt-a-whirl. Maybe I can outrun this dream, wake up and be home. Home hasn't sounded so good in years. Just the thought of it springs tears to my eyes, like a first time sleepaway camper lying in her bunk.

"Hey," someone says. I keep moving, a shark through water. "Some camera you got there." I catch sight of him out of the corner of my eye—an old man leaning against the doorjamb of a dilapidated shop. The window is chock-a-block with cameras—cool vintage ones, some of them versions of the one around my neck. "Can I have a look-see?" he says.

I'm out of breath—all the adrenaline. It feels good to pause for a moment and let my heart calm, as much as it can. "It's a Leica," I say, stepping closer to him.

"Don't I know it?" he says, shaking his head as though he were lucky to even lay eyes on the thing. He lets out a long whistle. "It's a beaut. Haven't seen one like this since the war. The other war," he corrects himself. "Interested in selling it?"

"No," I tell him. "Never."

"Gotcha. Say no more. You okay?" he asks. "You look a little peaked. Are you lost?"

"No, I'm fine," I insist. "It's 1967, right?"

"That's right. You sure you're okay?"

"I'm okay. It's 1967, and I'm just fine." He looks at me strangely. Who can blame him? I nod as if to reassure him that I'm a sane person, or more like, to reassure myself.

"Come back if you change your mind about the camera," he says, and then, an afterthought, "or if you need anything. I'm always right here."

I continue down Haight, then start weaving up and down the side streets, searching for something, anything familiar. Frankly, I don't even care what time or place it happens to be from. And then my eyes land on a VW van parked about a block off Haight. There's a Mandala decal plastered on the rear window.

∾

The sound of a band playing in fits and starts filters out to the street—short bursts of a song starting over and over again. Twangy guitar, tambourine, drums coming in a beat too late. I head toward the van parked in front of one of those Victorian gingerbread houses, all bay windows and gables, eons of wear and tear and chipped paint. Depending on the prospective buyer, my mother would either say it was oozing with charm or a teardown. The music is coming from that house.

I peer into the van. It's Jimmy's for sure. All the same crap—the batik curtains, the bag of nuts and raisins Jennifer chomped in my ear, that stupid prism dangling from the rearview mirror. I dig in my backpack for a scrap of paper to leave a note. Nothing other than a receipt from when Sarah and I went out for sushi last weekend and the iTunes gift card my

81

aunt gave me for Christmas. I turn over the scrap from Asakuma and start writing.

Mari Caldwell here. I'm the girl...

But I can't think of how to finish that sentence. I'm the girl who...what? What girl am I? I'm the girl who woke up to find herself back in time and you gave me a ride? I think not. I head up the path to the front door and knock.

A young woman opens the door, maybe nineteen or twenty years old. Her hair is parted down the middle, long and wild and dark. Her heavy, straight-across bangs brush her eyes, but you can still see those eyes have a don't-fuck-with-me hard edge. "Yeah?" she says, like it's a dare.

"I'm looking for...I mean, is this where...?" Suddenly I think I should have tried harder with the note option. I start again, stammering, "This band picked me up. A guy named Jimmy?"

On cue, Jimmy appears at the door. "Mari-Tamara-Caldwell!" he says as though we're old friends and it's perfectly acceptable, expected actually, for him to make fun of me in a friendly kind of way, as though it were our little routine.

"I'm sorry I just showed up here unannounced and all," I say. "But the thing is...Funny thing, I can't quite articulate the thing about the thing...Forget it. Sorry to have bothered you, to the extent that opening the door was a bother. I'll be leaving now. I mean, I don't even know you."

Jimmy smiles. "Sure you do. I'm the guy who got you across the bridge." He takes me by the arm, his hand gently gripping my upper arm, and leads me into the house. The weird thing is I can catch my breath when his hand is on my arm, guiding me in, but the instant he lets go, I am my old, adrenalized, shaky, poundy heart self. I can feel the brain chatter flooding back. It flies out of my mouth willy-nilly.

"This has been a really bad couple of days. I'm not sure how many actually. I got an Incomplete in Photog. Ridiculously unfair, I might add. Totally random on my teacher's part. Especially since, like, photography is actually sort of my thing. I had a total...you know, high drama scene with my mom. My laptop got a virus, and I forgot to reinstall the firewall so I blew all kinds of data. And clearly I forgot to charge my phone even though I so thought I did, and you know how it's like you're walking around without a limb when you don't have your phone. My fingers actually started to twitch a little 'cause I couldn't text my friend Sarah. There really must be something to that whole brain-nervous system connection. Suffice it to say...major withdrawal. And then I saw this newspaper...Kablooey!" I raise my hands to my temples and fling open my fingers to mimic the explosion in my brain.

"I have no idea what you just said," says Jimmy.

"I'm just really confused."

"It's okay," says Jimmy. "You're here now."

I can tell he's just trying to soothe me even though he probably thinks I'm nuts, or *because* he thinks I'm nuts. Either way, it's working.

CHAPTER
7

ONCE, IN elementary school, a girl in my class had a birthday party at a dollhouse museum that was in an old Victorian house. It was like the Russian dolls of Victorian dollhouses, being a dollhouse exhibit in a real Victorian house. The docent gave us this whole patter about how the rooms were originally used. The room I find myself entering, the room where the guys are rehearsing, would have been the parlor, or the drawing room, maybe even the music room, which is kind of apt since that's how these guys are using it now.

Jimmy guides me in, his hand on my elbow. Boo-Boo is pounding on his drums while P.J. plucks at his bass and Sam struggles with some licks on the guitar. Jennifer lies splayed on the couch—an ancient maroon number, tufted velvet, giving up its stuffing in random patches. Jennifer is weaving something out of yarn and twigs, resting it on her pregnant belly. She looks up from her arts and crafts long enough to smile at me. "You've got to stay," she says. "There's plenty of room. Right, Nina?"

So that's Nina. She shoots Jennifer a look. I intercept it mid-air as though I were a dirty look ninja. Nina says, "Are we starting a band or running a crash pad?" When she first opened the door, I figured this girl's giant, industrial sized attitude had to be all show, but I guess not.

Jennifer goes back to her weaving: yarn over and around, over and around. It's some sort of four-pointed thing. She reaches into the giant tote bag next to her and offers me a ball of multi-colored yarn. "You can make God's-eyes with me."

"It's cool," says Jimmy. "Stay with us."

"I can't stay here," I protest. "I've got to get home!"

All of a sudden, home is not just a place. It's not just my mother and my room and Sarah, but it's all this stuff I've got to do. "This is my crucial summer," I say. "I don't know if you go to college, or if you care about college, but I do. It's all I've been focused on for absolute ever. And if I don't spend every single day of this summer making sure my applications are perfect, then everything I've worked for my whole life will be useless. For one thing, I've got to take this stupid picture. Remember, I told you about the whole Incomplete debacle? So I've got to get home and take a portrait picture. I've got to check that off the list!" The tsunami of my to-do list washes over me. I swallow hard, but my voice cracks anyway.

"Settle down! One thing at a time," says Jimmy. "First of all, lists—who needs them? Secondly, where is home exactly?"

"That's the thing. I'm not sure. I mean, of course I know where…It's more like I'm not sure about when."

"Heavy, man," says Sam, tuning his guitar.

Nina shakes her head.

I've spent my lift cultivating the fine art of not caring what people think of me, but for some reason—some ridiculous, asinine reason—I care about what this Jimmy guy thinks of me, and I don't want him to think I'm a freak. A certifiable freak. Though it is pretty clear that any sort of standout freakishness would be hard to achieve with this bunch. I try to clarify. "Home is across the bridge. At least it used to be."

"I bet if you make a God's-eye, you'll remember where you live," says Jennifer. "God's-eyes have the power to see things that are unknowable by the physical eye."

"I'll take you," Jimmy says.

"We've got a lot of rehearsing to do," Nina pipes in. She conspicuously doesn't look at him.

Jimmy waves his hand through the air dismissively. "There's plenty of time," he says.

Nina looks at Jimmy for a long moment, but says nothing. Scary nothing. I look from Nina to Jimmy, Jimmy to Nina. And feel the blood drain from my face. I begin to wobble like a big-headed bobblehead; the more I fight the woozies, the stronger they attack.

"She doesn't look so good," says Jennifer, still weaving her yarn thing—purple over yellow, yellow over purple.

"When was the last time you ate something?" Jimmy asks.

"I don't know," I say. "Yesterday maybe? This morning? I think yesterday was this morning. "

Boo-Boo tosses his drumsticks over his shoulder with great aplomb. "I got the munchies myself."

"Me, too," P.J. chimes in.

"I could eat," says Sam.

Nina turns on her heels and marches out of the room.

CHAPTER

8

THERE IS actually a place called the Psychedelic Shop. Some sort of hippie general store. I pause to check out the window as we—the band guys and me—make our way down Haight. Liquid lettering swirls its way around posters—words camouflaged as flames and hair and sunbursts—vibrating with color against color. Pyrotechnic graphics. There are books and magazines, incense and bongs, sheepskin vests and beaded leather headbands, posters and records—the vinyl kind. And people. Live people, human mannequins but not frozen, just living in the window, looking out at the people looking in at them.

P.J. spews his joke as we make our way down the block. "So the guy, the explorer, he sees this huge neon sign, Himalaya Restaurant! He stumbles in and grabs a seat. The waiter rushes over and asks him what he wants. 'Anything! Bring me anything!' Dig it; the guy's wild starving. And the waiter says, 'How about Shlemma Pie? It's the specialty of the house.' 'Sure, sure, Shlemma Pie.' So the waiter brings him this

Shlemma Pie and the guy can't believe it. It's the best thing he's ever tasted. It's freakin' amazing. Like wow!"

The decibel level of P.J.'s voice gives me a headache. Or maybe my head just aches. I run two fingers over the goose eggs at my hairline. They are smaller, more speed bumps than hills, but still tender. I haven't looked in a mirror in…in however long it's been. I suspect these contusions have transitioned from red to purple to that final, if hideous, bruise mustard color. *I must be having some sort of crazy dream,* I think to myself, but it turns out I actually say it out loud because Jimmy nods. He says, "Yeah, isn't it cool?"

"Whatever," I say. "I'm going to wake up and it's all going to be over. It feels like I should remember you. I think I'll remember you. But I won't. You'll disappear by the time I brush my teeth."

"You'll remember what you need to," he assures me. He runs his hand through that chuck of hair that flops onto his forehead, brushing it back, but it just flops back down. And there's that smile again. I can't imagine ever forgetting that smile, how that smile makes pinpricks of heat pop on the surface of my skin.

We enter, en masse, a place called the Pall Mall Lounge. A sign in the window: a hand-drawn heart with an arrow bolting through it diagonally. Inside the heart, block printing hawks the Loveburger— twenty-five cents.

"Twenty-five cents!" I say. "Are they kidding?"

Jimmy pats me on the back, "Don't worry. They'll give it to you for free if you plead poverty."

"I could really use a Nonfat Venti Caramel Macchiato, extra foam," I say. "Preferably soy."

Jimmy stares at me, waiting for a translation.

"Coffee," I say.

"Coffee they got."

I brush against his arm on our way in the door and those tiny pinpricks fuse into one whole-body flush.

The place is just a five-stool lunch counter. A little boy—about nine, maybe ten—slides a spatula under a burger on the flattop. He flips it onto the bottom half of a bun and gives it a squirt of ketchup. Then he places the top half of the bun on the whole greasy mess and hands it over to a girl no older than me, a girl who looks like she hasn't had an encounter with a bar of soap in several days. Horrible epiphany moment: neither have I.

"Thanks," she says, wolfing it down.

"You're welcome," says the little boy. "Enjoy."

No money exchanges hands. Not even the lousy twenty-five cents scribbled on the sign. The boy tosses another patty onto the grill. The sizzle makes my stomach growl. I didn't even know I was hungry, let alone starving. "I do red meat rarely," I say. "Pun intended."

Jimmy takes a stool and pats the one next to him. I sit. The other guys huddle at the far end of the counter. It makes me kind of nervous to be sitting here with Jimmy as though it were a date or something, which it obviously is not. Nervous enough that I feel a ramble coming on. I direct all my energy to keeping my mouth shut and just letting these thoughts unspool, unspoken, in my head. Like about how the food storage conditions in this place do not appear all too sanitary, or haven't they ever heard of child labor laws, or how they're going to be really sorry they haven't collected people's quarters when the recession hits. I manage to keep it all in while Jimmy orders a burger for himself and one for me. Again, there's that itch. The itch to say something snarky. About how I can order for myself, thank you very much. But I don't. I don't say it. I just sit there, trying not to be so hyper-aware of the palpable sensation generated by Jimmy's simply sitting on the stool next to mine.

"Got it," says the little boy after Jimmy orders.

I stop him before he turns back to the grill. "Can I get a cup of coffee?" I ask, proud of myself for not Starbucking my order.

"Sure thing," he says. He pours the coffee into a thick crockery mug. A hairline crack zigzags across its surface and there's a hefty chip out of the lip. The boy puts down a shot glass sized pitcher—thick, ribbed glass filled with what must be heavy cream. I pour it into my coffee and the coffee turns the most wonderful color, deep caramel. It tastes great, too. Smoother, richer, way more comforting than when

I choke down a two percent latte. I wrap my hands around the mug and give in to its warmth.

At the other end of the counter, P.J. says, "He's a God."

"He may actually be God," Boo-Boo comments.

"It does kind of make one not even want to bother," says Sam.

The other two nod.

"They say he opened his show with Sgt. Pepper two days after the album was released," says Boo-Boo.

"Hendrix," says P.J. worshipfully.

"Hendrix," Sam concurs as though the name constituted a full sentence.

I think about telling them that Jimi's not long for this world. I can't remember exactly how old he was or what year it was when he died, but I know he burnt out pretty quickly. But I don't tell them. It would either sound too crazy or be too cruel or both. Enjoy the music while you can, boys. God's not long for this world.

Counter Boy refills my mug. "Wow!" he says, nodding toward the window. "Check it out!"

I glance over my shoulder. Past the other customers waiting for seats, past the storefront, past the lunatic mob scene on the sidewalk, I spot an old school bus lumbering down the road, a psychedelic paint job writhing its way across every square inch. A voice bellows from a loudspeaker: "You're either on the bus or you're off the bus!"

I can barely make out the bodies inside, but then I see that they are dancing, their faces painted green and Day-Glo orange. A sign across the front of the bus declares its destination—neither Nob Hill nor the Richmond District nor even Berkeley. In rococo printing across the top is one word: Furthur.

CHAPTER

9

OF COURSE, I've heard of these things. Love-Ins and Be-Ins and all that, but now that I think about it, I always assumed the whole peace-and-love thing had been exaggerated for the sake of myth. My parents' generation, the Baby Boomers, likes to fan the flames of hype about their youth as though they invented youth itself. As though they were the only group who ever got it right. As though it weren't so pathetic that they still think they're young.

But this scene in the park is for real. A crowd stretching as far as I can see, a proverbial sea of people that ebbs and flows as though a collective spell has been cast.

Full-on Fellini circus. A surge of pulsing colors. Banners and flags wave in the sunshine. Balloons hover overhead, punctuating the sky. Food appears— hunks of bread, along with giant cookies and wine. You can smell the wine, fruity and earthy and like vinegar. So much skin: human canvases painted with flowers and peace symbols. Naked toddlers finger paint each other with mud, pausing to suck on a bare breast now and then. A girl in a see-through dress prances around a guy cross-legged on the ground playing guitar. A couple is hooking up—right there—under a thin parachute, a tangle of denim cast to the side. The sun flashes off a dress made of foil as the breeze whips beaded fringe dangling from ponchos and jackets and high suede boots.

Someone in the distance is blowing giant soap bubbles; they rise over the park, shimmering and iridescent. Ribbons extending from a pole sail over the crush of people, the pole topped with a peace symbol made to look like stained glass. Which seems fitting, because there's this surreal ceremonial feel to the whole scene, like a field of woodland nymphs has crawled out of the bushes and gathered to participate in some tribal ritual, bits and pieces of pagan sacraments jumbled together, presided over by self-imagined shamans.

And with so much music. Flutes and guitars. Mandolins and dulcimers. Bells and cymbals and gongs. Drums pounding out what I suppose can only be called, more than a little nauseatingly, a communal heartbeat.

Suddenly, a long, drawn-out sound pierces the air. A trumpet, maybe. No, nothing brass. There's nothing sharp to the sound. And not a woodwind. Just a single note. More like a tone, echoing over the crowd, the pitch wavering ever so slightly. For a second, I think it's a recording of a whale—a whale calling to his fellow pod members deep underwater. But that's not it. Someone, somewhere in this human pod, is blowing a conch shell.

And then, a long, protracted "Om" over the loudspeaker. No cosmic key left unturned.

"Welcome to America's nervous breakdown!" booms a voice from the stage. Cheers. Hollers. Applause. An enormous American flag waves high above the throng. In place of stars: a giant peace symbol.

Whoa.

"Sell your radios!" the speaker continues. "We are face-to-face with the dawning of a new epoch. Cancel your subscriptions. Tune into that other band of consciousness that broadcasts love and joy!"

Double whoa!

I'm not a big crowd person—that is to say, I'm not big on crowds, and the two cups of coffee have kicked in so that I'm already feeling a little snaggy by the time we make our way into the heart of the park, into the eye of this bizarre collective Cirque Du Soul. There must be thousands of people here, tens of thousands maybe.

Jimmy leads the way as we wade through the sea of undulating bodies, and believe me, "undulating" is not a word I use haphazardly. Everyone's moving to the music of the band on stage. Tie-dyed speaker covers seem to pulsate with the bass guitar. The lead singer looks kind of familiar—long, dark hair. I think it might be Jerry Garcia, a very young, clean-shaven Jerry Garcia. I try to picture his caricature on a pint of Cherry Garcia, but all I can remember are bright red cherries, turquoise sky, and a bunch of puffy clouds. Maybe Ben and Jerry couldn't buy the rights to his face, even with all their high-fat millions. Jerry's long dead. (Another one, like Jimi…got to keep my mouth shut about that. I'd hate to be trapped in the middle of a communal buzzkill of such gargantuan proportion.) Anyway, maybe Garcia's posthumous "people" were asking for some humongous sum of money for the privilege of plastering his face on an ice cream carton, so Ben and Jerry said screw that and opted for cherries and clouds and, now that I think of it, a cow.

Somebody offers me a mugful of coagulated something—stew of some kind, smelling of cabbage and sweat socks, the muddy color of one crayon too many. I decline the glop, saying to no one in particular, "Give me a break."

"You should try being a little more open-minded," Jimmy says, raising his voice over the din.

"Yeah, well, you can be so open-minded that your brains fall out," I say. Cheap shot. Whatever.

"Sometimes, Mari-Tamara-Caldwell…" he looks at me hard. "Sometimes you've just got to go with the flow."

I hold his gaze, determined not to fall into it. "I don't do flow. Flow is highly overrated."

"But the fun part is," he says, "you never know where it will take you."

Someone grabs hold of my hand. I try to break free, but the grip conveys all the energy of all the other hands holding the hand holding my hand. There is no resisting. I am swept into the human daisy chain snaking its way through the park. I turn to Jimmy: Help! He grasps my other hand, an anchor in the mayhem, an anchor to some version of reality. I have no idea which version that might be, but there does seem to be some sort of real when he holds my hand, some sort of real that's convincingly non-dreamlike.

Another voice from the stage: "This gathering of the tribes is just beginning! We're going to keep gathering and keep growing and keep believing until we prove to the establishment…" He actually says "establishment." The human chain stops in its path to listen as he gains steam. "We are going to prove to the establishment once and for all: bombs won't change the world. Love will change the world!"

I roll my eyes—reflex. But Jimmy is nodding his agreement, and for just a moment, I envy him the luxury of such unfettered believing.

"You know that moment when you hold the needle over the record, and then you drop it?" he says. "That split second before the needle hits the groove?"

I don't tell him technology has left vinyl in its dust. There's no point.

"This is like that moment," he says. "Full of anticipation for something wonderful, something that might change your life. But on a whole global scale."

Boo-Boo appears at our side, his arm draped around a girl wearing a floppy suede hat and a halter top, no more than a couple of strings of paisley fabric positioning two small triangles over her boobs. (I struggle to remember if the triangles are isosceles… shit…so much to review before the SAT's in the fall.) "It's all coming together, man," says Boo-Boo. "The planets are lining up."

"Total harmony," offers P.J.

"Right on!" whoops Sam.

"What is wrong with you people?" I say. "This is all bullshit." My moment of longing to catch Jimmy's wavelength and surf it to some sort of cosmic optimism has definitely passed. I look at these guys and actually pity them. "Can't you see this is just a dream? You're all just dreaming."

"Somebody has to," says Jimmy.

"Yeah," I say, "and when you wake up in forty years, you know what you're going to do? Go online and check your portfolio."

They're staring at me now, but I'm on a roll. "All you're going to care about is how much money you're making. It's all about money. Always has been, always will be."

"Dig it," says Sam. "Chick's plugged into the conspiracy."

"It's not a conspiracy!" I shriek. "It's just growing up and giving up and just plain human nature. It's ordinary people living for their Lexus and their gigantor flat screen and saving up to get their thighs liposuctioned."

"Huh?" Boo-Boo scrunched up his face.

"Lipo—getting the fat sucked out."

Boo-Boo takes a step back, away from me.

"Are you okay?" Jimmy asks. "Is there something wrong?"

Of course, he's thinking: Is there something wrong *with me?* Like pathologically. But I can't stop. "Yes, there's something wrong," I say. "Actually, everything's wrong. Wake up and smell the herbal tea. You're all going to grow up to be your parents!"

P.J. recoils. "Low blow!"

"It's the truth. You grew up to be my parents. I mean, not my parents specifically..." Yikes! Is that possible? That would be a little too Marty McFly, wouldn't it? I shake off the notion with a shiver, but can't quite shake off the epiphany that goes with it—that my parents were like this once, full of hope and buoyancy, full of confidence in their ability to change the world, full of faith in their ability to love each other. And now...now, they're so not. "What I mean is, you're going to be exactly like my parents. Everyone will, except for, like, a few psychos living in cabins in Wyoming or some godforsaken place where they end up going postal or stocking a freezer full of body parts that pair nicely with fava beans and a nice Chianti."

Boo-Boo turns to Jimmy. "What'd you give her, man? She's freakin' out."

"I am not," I announce, summoning all shreds of sanity. "I'm just out of time."

"For what?" asks Jimmy. "What is it you need to do?"

"Listen to me! I'm not out of time. I'm out of my time. You don't get it. How could you possibly? I don't get it. I've gone through some kind of black hole and come out the other side." I sweep my hand in front of them all. "You're all on the other side. Or else I'm just stuck in a bend in the road of a cosmic time warp."

Sam shakes his head. "She must have had some bad shit."

Jimmy takes my face in his hand, lowers his face so that it's inches from mine and looks me in the eye. "Who gave you that stuff?"

I try to catch my breath. Finally saying it out loud—the crazy time travel stuff—supercharged me. My heart isn't pumping right; it's stuck on squeeze and is skipping release. Just squeezing tighter, tighter. And now the feel of Jimmy's hands on my cheeks, a perfect fit for my face. Heart squeezing tighter. This can't be normal. It's like someone's trying to turn my heart from a lump of coal into a diamond.

"You're too young for that shit," Jimmy says.

"Too young?" I say. "Too young! You have no idea! I'm not even born yet!"

P.J. nods sympathetically. "I feel that way sometimes."

I manage to take a step back from Jimmy. "You're not listening to me. Somehow or other, I've gone back in time. I don't belong here. I'm from the future."

Jimmy considers the possibility. When he finally speaks, his voice is soft and measured. He's going with the option that I'm out of my mind, a not unreasonable deduction. "Mari," he says, dropping the Mari-Tamara-Caldwell thing, "Of course you went back in time. Everybody does that now and then. Everything will be fine, let's just relax…" I can tell he doesn't mean a word. He's just pacifying me, like he's reciting from the manual on how-to-talk-someone-off-the-ledge-of-bad-drugs.

"Don't pretend. I know you don't believe me," I say, agitated and speedy, kind of making the bad drugs point for him.

"Listen to yourself," Jimmy says, mentally turning to the next page in the manual. "I don't really know, of course, but I'm not sure it's possible to go back in time."

Sam shoots Jimmy a look. Could very well be possible as far as he's concerned.

"What's the use?" I say. "I don't believe it myself."

Boo-Boo muses aloud. "Maybe she did some of that Orange Sunshine. Eddie from Pismo got hold of that shit and didn't come down for three days. Got himself arrested running naked through the Panhandle."

"Given my control issues," I say, "as in I like to maintain control at all costs, I would never touch the stuff." Clearly, they don't believe me. There's no explaining that my doors of perception have been flung open without any chemical assistance.

"I'll get over to Bear's and score some downers," P.J. volunteers.

"We could take her to that new place…" says Boo-Boo.

"The Free Clinic," Sam provides the name.

"Yeah," says Boo-Boo. "I hear they're pretty good at dealing with freak-outs. And they're free."

They all look at him. Duh.

"Let's start by getting her some coffee," says Jimmy.

"No," I say. I wish I could rewind all the babble that just flooded out of me. Normally, I wouldn't care, but I don't want these guys to think I'm tripping or that I'm nuts. "I just bumped my head really hard. I'll be better in the morning."

"Yeah," says Jimmy. "You need a good night's sleep. Things always look better in the morning."

"I've got to figure out how to get home," I say. Now that I've said it, I want it more than anything.

"We can figure that out tomorrow," he answers.

I shake my head no. Tomorrow seems too far away to wait for. I don't know if I can make it to tomorrow. Tears well in my eyes, even though I don't really do crying. I make a point of it. In fact, I can't remember crying since I stood in the doorway three years ago watching my father's Range Rover pull out of the driveway and disappear beyond the hedges. Crying is so lame, so humiliating. But somehow when Jimmy reaches over to wipe away the single tear creeping down my cheek, I'm not all that embarrassed.

"There's always tomorrow," he says simply.

CHAPTER
10

I SPOT her as we approach the house. Nina—curled up in the window seat of the old Victorian, peering out from behind the frayed lace curtains yellowed with age and dingy with smoke. I can pinpoint the moment she catches sight of us trooping down Belvedere. She lets go the curtains and scrambles from the seat. It's dusk by now, the sky turning from mauve to gray, but I can make out her silhouette as it shifts from sitting, her face obscured by the curtains, to standing. The lace ruffles back into place against the glass.

Jimmy's hand rested gently on my shoulder the whole time we've been walking back from the park. It's nothing more than a protective gesture, sort of a big brotherly thing, I'm sure. He doesn't want me to pass out on his watch or anything melodramatic like that. I'm not going to lie, however, I don't mind that Nina may have noticed his hand on me and kind of hope she's having a hard time getting her game face back on.

Apparently not.

By the time we all barge into the parlor, she's loaded for bear, as my father would say.

"What the fuck?" barks Nina. "We were supposed to be rehearsing today."

"Easy," says Jimmy, holding up his two hands, palms forward, the universal gesture of back off.

Nina is not so easily cooled. "You morons have wasted a whole day."

"You should've come," says P.J. "The scene in the park was amazing!"

"We've been waiting for this chance all year," Nina spits out. "I've been waiting for this chance my whole life." She storms out of the parlor through the dining room where the prisms dangling from the funky old crystal chandelier throw sunset shadows across the walls. Nina keeps moving, on into the kitchen at the back of the house. She flings closed the kitchen door. It is one of those old-fashioned swinging doors, and she pushes it with such force that it keeps swinging, squeaking itself back and forth. It's the only sound in the house as the guys gaze after Nina's trail, transfixed by the sheer intensity of her exit.

I perch on the arm of the sofa, barely keeping my eyes open and pretending not to study Jimmy for his reaction. Finally, Jimmy gives a little shrug and turns to me. "What you need is sleep," he says and he heads upstairs, motioning me to follow. Which I do. I follow him like a puppy; who am I all of a sudden?

I slide my hand up the banister—mahogany, I think—with curlicue carvings, the repeating pattern guiding me up the stairs in my stupor. A hallway extends from the top of the stairs to the back of the house. Jimmy makes his way down the hall without checking to see that I'm still behind him. He knows I am.

The last room on the left is shabby and small, less than half the size of my room at home. Crumbles of plaster lie on the floor beneath a hole in the ceiling where a waterlogged patch has given up holding on. I assume black mold, or another virulent spore, must be lurking up there. The wallpaper, peeling in random patches, is a maze of vines punctuated with cabbage roses. Clots of glue mottle the surface. A child's school desk, vintage even for the sixties, is pushed against one wall, the name Sally etched deeply into the upper right corner. A single bed is shoved against another wall; a chenille bedspread—dusty rose in color—bunches at its foot.

Jimmy smoothes the bedspread, pulling it up, then away from the bed, like opening an envelope for me to slide into. He cocks his head toward the bed. Having eschewed all those dumb parties in middle school where prepubescent couples get locked in closets for seven minutes or whatever they do, I have never actually been in a bedroom alone with a guy. Let alone a guy who looks like this and is holding the covers back for me.

I sit on the edge of the bed, but I'm so exhausted. If I lie down, will he think I'm…I don't know… consenting to whatever? Am I? I might be. But mostly, I'm so tired. Too tired not to lie down. I rummage in my brain for a snide crack that might defuse the situation as I slip under the covers, but I can't access any snark. Like something, someone, has cleared the history on my brain.

I curl onto my side as Jimmy draws the quilt up and rests it gently on my shoulders like a whisper. He bends over me for a moment to adjust the blanket. He smells of something spicy, maybe cinnamon…no… cloves, and slightly of sweat, which would normally be gross, but on him, seems to work. My heart does that squeezy thing again, but in a good way this time. I feel his breath on my neck as he leans over me and my chin tilts up a little, involuntarily, to expose more neck to feel more breath. My breathing shifts to the rhythm of his breathing as his face hovers inches above me.

I wish I knew what you're supposed to do at a moment like this. I wish I were one of those girls who knew how to do something that didn't appear to be anything, anything at all, but that made you irresistible. I've watched those girls, observed them working their subterranean magic. I've taken photos that catch them in the act—flipping their hair over a shoulder, tilting their heads at a just-so angle, smiling without agenda, giggling. Photos that make me shake my head in confusion at the whole mating dance. Not for me. *Au contraire.* Now, suddenly, I wish I were one of those girls. I wish I knew a step or two of that dance. Given all that's happened to me, it's pretty demented, but the impulse to want Jimmy to like me—to "like" me like me—turns out to be the biggest surprise of all. Not that it matters. Who am I kidding? Why would he? Who would, let alone him? All he's doing is tucking me in.

He crosses to a raggedy overstuffed easy chair in the corner, plops himself down, releasing a puff of dust. He switches off a yellow glass lamp etched with flowers, a paisley scarf draped over its cracked shade. Who knows why, but the darkness seems to prove this is not a dream. If it were, my fingers wouldn't come upon this bald patch in the nubby chenille. If it were, the smell of bergamot lingering on the comforter wouldn't tingle my nostrils. If it were, Jimmy would have kissed me…even though I can't begin to dream of what that would feel like.

Truth is I've never been kissed. Four summers ago at camp, Justin McCord did something resembling a kiss to me. Note: he did it *to* me, not *with* me. It was meant to be a kiss, but it ended up being some weird lip-to-cheek grazing. When I told Sarah about it, we agreed that while intent may be nine-tenths of the law, you need a full ten-tenths when it comes to making out. At the very least, you need lip-to-lip contact. Only Sarah knows that I'm about to be

a senior in high school and I've never been kissed.
At first, I didn't believe her when she told me that
Michael Rathgar kissed her—actually fully made out
with her—while watching the most recent James
Bond movie, no less. I think it was *Casino Royale*. But
when I gave her claim some consideration, I realized
she was probably telling the truth because: a) why
would she lie to me of all people? and b) Sarah and
I are both what you might call James Bond purists,
which makes us welcome any distraction—even
making out with Michael Rathgar—while being
subjected to post-Sean Connery Bond. So...that
leaves me. Unkissed.

Long-winded explanation as to why I'm a little
annoyed Jimmy doesn't kiss me. (Confession: I've
perfected the art of turning disappointment into
annoyance.) What's wrong with me anyway? Despite
my effort to hide it, you can hear the pissed-off in my
voice when I say, "You don't have to babysit me."

"I can use the peace and quiet," he says. "I've got
a song to write." He lifts the guitar leaning against
the chair and begins to pick out a tune. I normally
have all kinds of sleep-inducing rituals, little games
I play in my brain to make it turn off, but tonight
I feel myself drifting off immediately. I will my eyes
open, not ready to let go. Even though he didn't kiss
me, even though he's sitting over there and I'm lying
here, even though I'm just the kid he drove across
the bridge, I want to hang onto the two of us alone in

this room. I prop my head up on one hand and watch him scribble on a scrap of paper between strumming chords tentatively shaping themselves into a melody.

"You looked good up on that stage," I say.

"What?"

"At the Fillmore. You looked like you belonged there."

"You were watching me?"

I don't answer.

"I was watching you, too," he says.

"You were?"

I think he's just being nice. Or else going out of his way to embarrass me, but he doesn't seem like that kind of person. Besides, I generally do a more than adequate job of that myself.

"It was pretty intense how you were watching everything. Observing," he says. "You knew exactly when to take the picture."

"Really?"

"Absolutely. To capture the essence of the moment. I bet the pictures are going to be great."

"I hope so," I said. "I need a really great one. To wipe out that Incomplete."

"For school?"

I nod.

"Don't worry about taking pictures for some class. Take the pictures you want to."

I want to take pictures that will buy me Early Decision to Yale, but I won't admit it. Besides, when

I think about it, there's more to it. I actually do want to take great pictures, Yale or no Yale.

"Is that why you write music?" I ask. "Just because you want to?"

"Is there a better reason?"

"I guess not."

"I write songs because I want to," he says. "And because I need to. I wouldn't be me if I didn't."

"All that stuff about changing the world," I say, "do you seriously believe it?"

"Absolutely." He seems so sure. "Maybe not the whole world at once. Maybe with one heart at a time."

In ordinary life, that would be such a straight line. But this is not ordinary life and my snark reflex is still disabled. I let my head settle back onto the pillow. And I say nothing. Nothing at all.

CHAPTER
11

"GET UP off that throne, boy."

I startle awake to the sound of Nina's voice. For a moment I'm not sure where I am. Feels like I'm at Sarah's and her little sister has barged in to annoy us. But then I remember. And I miss Sarah. I'll never be able to describe these freakazoids to her. And even if I could describe Jimmy, I could never describe the way it felt when he was leaning over me in bed last night. Like I wanted to give in, instead of having something to prove. I close my eyes and try to conjure the feeling, but Nina's voice cuts through.

"I said, get up off that throne, boy," she says again.

She has interrupted Boo-Boo in the bathroom next to my room. (It took me a minute in the middle of the night to figure out that the flushing mechanism was one of those old-fashioned pull-chain thingies, like at that 1890's ice cream parlor where my parents used to take me to celebrate my birthday when I was little, back when the three of us could still sit around a table—even if it was a kitsch old-timey wrought iron thing—and actually laugh over hot fudge and clouds of whipped cream.)

The walls in this place are paper thin. I can hear Boo-Boo say, "I'm reading. It's the latest *Freak Brothers*."

"I don't care if it's *War and Friggin' Peace*. It's time to make some music." Nina's voice has that drill sergeant edge. I do not want that tone trained on me.

Nina slams the bathroom door and carries on corralling the boys. I figure it doesn't count as eavesdropping since she is making such a noisy show of the process.

P.J. is in his room listening to the stereo. He says exactly that, "Stereo, man..." as though lying on the floor with his head between two speakers is producing nirvana. He's not listening to Nirvana, of course— too soon by several decades, I think—although if he were, Kurt Cobain would be just another tragic dead disappointment.

"Get your ass downstairs," Nina commands.

P.J. mutters something else, but I can't make it out. I hear footsteps in the hall, then the creak of another door opening.

"You're hogging all the marshmallows, Sam," Jennifer says.

"Look who's talking. You're excavating for nuts," says Sam.

"Come on, Sam," Nina prods. "We've got work to do."

"Oooo," he says with exaggerated dread, "you said the 'w' word."

"Give Jennifer the damn rocky road and get yourself downstairs," says Nina.

I hold my breath, head hovering inches off the pillow the better to hear, waiting for Nina's order to Jimmy, but she heads downstairs. I counted the doors as I passed them last night, having unwittingly absorbed that habit from my mother-the-realtor. (She cannot set foot in a house without evaluating it as a potential listing.) I know there are no more bedrooms. Jimmy must be downstairs already.

I crawl out from under the comforter and tiptoe to the door. I close my eyes tight as though that will make the door creak less when I crack it open. I hear the guys heading downstairs and step back, hiding in the shadow of the door.

Downstairs, Jimmy asks, "Everyone present and accounted for?" No sarcasm, simply an ordinary question. Seems like straightforwardness warped over the decades. When did so much irony settle in? During the seventies? The nineties?

"How's the song coming?" asks Nina.

"Not quite there yet," says Jimmy.

"Well, maybe if you weren't so busy playing nursemaid to Little Miss Muffet, you'd get the damn thing written."

I hold my breath waiting for his response. What's he going to say about me? Nothing. "Don't worry about it," he says. "The song's on its way. It just hasn't arrived yet."

I close the door, the hinges squeaking obstinately. (Petulantly? I'll have to look up the difference before I take the next practice SAT.) This place is old even if it is forty-five years younger than it's supposed to be…or than I am. Thinking about that makes my brain clash against my skull. But I can't afford to waste brain power on anything other than a plan to get home. Short of dropping another book on my head or ramming a bicycle into a tree, I can't imagine what that plan might be. My dad always taught me to think outside the box, but my problem now is, having landed so far outside the box, how to get back in.

I slept long and hard, but ten more minutes might help. I crawl back into bed and pull the covers over my head like I usually do on Sunday mornings, especially when Patrick, my mother's dork-head boyfriend, has slept over and is flipping pancakes in the kitchen, usually while whistling. Once I told him, "Gee, thanks, but I'm a little old for Mickey Mouse pancakes," so he started making mine in the shape of an "M" for Mari. What does this guy have against ordinary circles anyway?

I'm almost drifting off—an almost dream of falling off a cliff, expecting to fly—when Nina bursts in.

"Good morning," she says, plunking herself down in the chair where Jimmy sat the night before. "He likes you."

"Who?"

"Don't be coy."

"He's just being nice," I say, but suddenly an entire habitat of butterflies unleashes in my stomach.

"Who do you think you're kidding?" says Nina. "I've got eyes. I can see what's going on."

Nina thinks she's so smart. Little does she know there's absolutely nothing going on. Or is there? Has she seen something that I'm missing because I'm…shall we say, inexperienced in such matters, a.k.a. supremely dense? I almost wish we were friends, Nina and I, so that we could have a heart-to-heart and I could quiz her for details and parse every little Jimmy glance.

Instead, I say, "Nothing's going on. I don't know what you're talking about." And then, as though I'm suddenly the star of a sophisticated romantic comedy, I add, "You can have him. He's all yours." My lids flutter a little because that seems like the proper stage direction for delivering a line like that.

"I have no use for Jimmy Westwood outside of the band," Nina shrugs.

"What about free love and all that?" I say, trying a less anachronistic movie line.

"Nothing's free, little girl," says Nina, "especially love. Love comes with the highest price of all. But nobody here is talking about love, so listen to me, sweet thing, and listen good 'cause I'm only going to tell you this once."

"I know," I say. "It's for my own good."

"Fuck your own good. All I care about is the band. You become Jimmy's little pet project and that'll be the end. I won't have you doing a number on him. The band will take a back seat and that'll be that."

"I told you," I say, "I'm not becoming anything. I was lost…"

"And now you're found," Nina interrupts. "How quaint. I got it the moment I laid eyes on you."

"I'm telling you…"

Nina holds up a hand to shush me. "And I'm telling you," she says. She gets up from the chair, her hair bouncing off her shoulders, and strides over to the bed where I sit hugging the pillow against my chest like a shield. Her face is no more than five inches from mine.

"Jimmy wrote a great song once. Only once. And that was when his heart was broken. He gets stupid when he's in love. That means no song. No band. No contract. No nothing. So do us all a favor and keep away from him."

My eyes widen, partly because Nina's just plain scary, and partly because I can't believe she thinks I could be an actual threat. Like romantically. I lower the pillow and look her in the eye. "All I want to do is go home."

She calls my bluff. "So what are you waiting for?"

There's no good answer to that question.

CHAPTER
12

THE AROMA of cookies baking fills downstairs. There's Jennifer in the kitchen, dusted in flour, combining oats and nuts and seeds in a huge pottery bowl. I tiptoe past and then past the parlor where Nina has wrangled the guys. Boo-Boo settles himself behind the drums; Sam straps on his guitar; P.J. strums his bass.

Jimmy scribbles on a piece of paper, then crumples it into a ball and chucks it. The floor is littered with false starts. I want to tell him I know he has a great song in him even though there's no way I'd really know that, never having heard anything he's written, including the one great song Nina told me about. I want to tell him I believe in him, which is so incredibly lame that I almost make myself gag. I'm beginning to see that this Jimmy thing is complicated. Nina, not so much. Jimmy or no Jimmy—I want nothing to do with that girl.

It may be 1967, but Nina has missed the go-with-the-flow train. She's so driven that she might as well be…well, from the present. My present, that is. The mind reels at what she'd accomplish with a computer at her disposal. Weirdly, much as she scares me, I feel kind of sorry for her. She's smack in the middle of a cultural tide that's going to become the stuff of legends, if rather overblown, and she's swimming against the current (to torture an aquatic metaphor). It must be exhausting. Or, on the other hand, not as exhausting as pretending not to care what people think of you. I guess we're sort of similar in that respect. But she manages the charade without all my stupid verbal tap dancing. She says what's on her mind and orders people around and stomps out of rooms. I kind of admire that, I guess. But that doesn't mean I want to be around her. No, I'm out of here. I grab my backpack and tiptoe out the front door as I hear Nina call the guys to order with a whack of the tambourine.

I head north on Belvedere to Haight where I turn right, away from the park. I pass a place called the Persian Aub Zam Zam. I don't have time to figure out what that could possibly be. I need to get out of Hashbury and back to the bridge. I'll walk across the bridge if I have to. I just want to get home.

I edge my way through the crowd and continue down Haight, accosted by those ubiquitous posters—yellow and blue, pink and green, colors electrifying each other edge to edge beneath that bulbous, free-flowing font that's so…sixties. Why do all their letters have to ooze across the page to announce this band or that poetry reading? Don't these people know from a classic Helvetica?

I recognize a shop where I once bought a tie-dyed T-shirt, a hold-out from these days in my day. I was in the fifth grade and a classmate was throwing a hippie party. My mom brought me here. I narrowed it down to two: a mostly blue and green one and a rainbow one with a peace symbol on it. When I couldn't decide, my mom bought them both for me, then we caught a cab to the Fairmont and stuffed ourselves with puu-puus in the hotel's Polynesia-on-steroids Tonga Room. Halfway through my second Virgin Pina Colada, a fake rainstorm started and a band appeared on a tiki barge that floated out onto the pool in the middle of the room. My mom and I so didn't want to leave that we ordered another puu-puu platter. I ate crab rangoon until my whole self smelled of fried wonton and my fingertips were slick with grease. My mom called it a "girls' day out," which only makes sense when there's a man at home, conspicuously absent from the day, but not when he's gone from your entire household. I really wish my mom and I could go for another puu-puu fest right now.

I hail a taxi on the spot.

"Can you take me to Mill Valley?" I ask.

"I can if you got twenty bucks," says the driver, his mouth full of bagel and cream cheese. Gross.

I rummage in my backpack for my wallet. Inside it are six ones. "Hang on," I say. I remember passing a

Wells Fargo and take off down the street. I pull out my ATM card and fumble with some weird slot by the front door of the bank. It doesn't fit. Where are you supposed to slide your card?

A guard approaches me. "Can I help you, young lady?"

"I can't figure out how to use this ATM."

"What?" he asks.

"The money machine."

"This is a bank, young lady, not a money machine."

I study the slot again. "Night Deposit." Oh. The cop gives me the once-over. Is it possible this is a time before ATM's? I thought there were always ATM's. So anyone who thinks you can get money out of a wall must be on drugs, which seems to be the standard explanation for all manner of bizarre behavior. I laugh, like he and I are in on the joke together. The cop shakes his head as I head back down the street, merging into the crowd as quickly as possible.

I shove my wallet back into my backpack. My hand brushes against the crocodile surface of my Leica as I catch sight of the camera store. I run my fingers across the camera stowed deep in my backpack and wonder how much that old guy would give me for it. Ought to be at least a couple hundred dollars, maybe more. It's vintage and in mint condition. There must have been several rounds of inflation since then, I assume, so I recalculate. Even so, fifty dollars would get me across the bridge.

I'm not sure I can part with the Leica. It's a habit of mine to reach for the camera and run my hands across it, feeling its contours and its pebbly surface. Since time stopped working and dumped me in 1967, I find myself doing that more and more, at weird moments—not to take pictures, but sort of to remember there's something beyond myself. I'm connected, not only to my father and his father, but to all the experiences they had when they were holding it, all the places they saw and the people they met, all the things the camera ever photographed. It's kind of photography voodoo. It's not like I consciously formulate the thought every time I hold the thing, but it's definitely more than just a camera, and I can't imagine selling it. I wouldn't be me without it. But am I me in this crazy place and time? Should I start walking and head to the bridge, or am I meant to make some monumental sacrifice, like selling my camera, in order to get home?

"What you up to, Sunshine?" That voice, like loose gravel. It's that guy from the Fillmore—Royce, right there behind me.

"I'm trying to find a way home."

"C'mon," he says, placing a hand on my shoulder. "I got wheels."

I don't move.

"I don't bite," he says coolly, "...unless you want me to."

I roll my eyes. Oh please.

CHAPTER
13

ROYCE DRIVES a shiny black Mustang convertible. Naturally. It matches his leather pants. It would be so easy to get into this car and let him drive me across the bridge. There's no guarantee that across the bridge means home, but this side of the bridge sure doesn't. Of course, there's the distinct possibility that this guy could be a Charles Manson wannabe. I have no idea what year that whole wild-eyed Charlie thing happened, so, for that matter, this guy could actually *be* Charles Manson, amping up the whole Stranger Danger thing logarithmically.

"You're kind of a mystery, aren't you, Sunshine?" he says. Sunshine is precisely what a cult leader would call his little acolyte groupies.

"Me?" I say. "Actually, I'm quite boring. Seriously dull, if you want to know the truth. Yawnsville." He shoves his thumbs behind his filigreed belt buckle, a massive Wild West brass chunk of a thing, obviously just for show since his leather pants are so tight they couldn't possibly fall down.

"So where are you from exactly?" he says.

"Across the bridge."

"Not too far."

"Farther than you think," I say.

"You still got that camera on you?" he asks.

I nod.

"So let's stop by my place, and you can take my picture."

That is so not going to happen. Never let them take you to a second location; we've all had that lesson drummed into us.

"I'm not sure that's a good idea," I say. "I mean, I don't have the right film. Of course, everyone's waiting in line for that new Apple phone that's going to have a camera built in, but..." I stop myself, like someone visiting a foreign country who suddenly realizes she has lapsed back into her native tongue.

"It doesn't matter. Use whatever camera you like," says Royce. "I can't take a bad picture."

I could throw up. Instead, I improvise. "I think for what you're after...I'm assuming you need an album cover? I'd need Plus-X, and I've got Tri-X in the camera right now. Whole wrong ASA."

Royce opens the door to the car and places a very warm hand on the small of my back, with the slightest pressure. His hand slides down a few inches, greater pressure. Eeeww. However, getting into this car means I don't have to sell my camera. I could make a stab at getting home *and* keep my camera. Win-win. But full-of-himself guy in leather pants comes with the bargain, making it a little too Faustian for comfort.

I glance toward the camera shop, weighing my options, when I spot the guys: Boo-Boo, P.J., and Jimmy, bouncing out of the hardware store, toting cans of paint.

"My friends are over there!" I say, slamming the car door before taking off down the street.

"Hey!" Royce calls after me. I don't even turn around. I'm walking too fast toward Jimmy and the guys. Actually, I'm running.

"Jimmy!" I call out.

He spins on his heels and opens his arms wide to me. To *me*. The paint cans swing from their arch of wire handle. "Where'd you disappear to?" he asks, "and what the hell are you doing with that piece of trouble?" Behind me, I can hear Royce revving the Mustang's engine, its full-throated rasp mimicking his own, then squealing away from the curb—a vehicular Fuck You.

"You're just in time to help us," says P.J., saving me from answering Jimmy's question.

"We're painting the old homestead," Boo-Boo explains.

"I love to paint!" I say. Truth: I've never painted anything in my life, let alone a house. I grab one of the cans from Boo-Boo. We are heading back to the house, the opposite direction from the bridge. It doesn't matter. I'm just relieved to be rid of that

Royce guy. He's got a certain magnetism—he'd be the first to admit it—but bottom line: he's creepy.

Besides, the bridge isn't going anywhere. Painting the house will buy me a little extra time to get used to the idea of selling the camera. Or maybe Jimmy will drive me back. I'm sure all I'd have to do is ask. Of course, I don't even know what's on the other side of the bridge. All I know as I'm walking back to the house is that Jimmy's on this side.

❧

Turns out the guys had made a deal: painting the house in lieu of rent. They line up the cans on the front porch. P.J. removes the lids ceremoniously, one by one, revealing a color palette that is not exactly a palette, but more of a rainbow: goldenrod, chartreuse, shocking pink, violet. Nina comes out of the house, stands over the cans, hands on hips. "What the fuck?"

"Listen," says Boo-Boo, "the landlord said we had to paint the place. He didn't say what color."

The guys devolve into a swarm of preschoolers turned loose with a new set of finger paints. P.J. rolls cobalt blue over an expanse of wall, while Boo-Boo finesses the trim with canary yellow. Sam dips a finer brush into the hot pink and dabs at the intricate scrollwork on one of the four columns that stand guard outside the house. More paint splatters onto the ground than the house, but they're into it.

Nina, the frustrated den mother, retreats inside. Paint fumes give her a migraine, she claims. Basically, Nina is a walking migraine. She's wound so tight you can see this throbbing vein that runs vertically down the side of her neck, a little too close to the surface. When the boys don't behave, the vein looks like it's going to spurt. Or, and I don't think I'm imagining this, when Jimmy looks at me. In fact, the precise moment she claims migraine is when Jimmy asks me to hold the ladder for him. If a person were so inclined, a person could make a connection.

"My life is in your hands," says Jimmy as he reaches the top of the ladder, clutching a can of violet paint.

"I won't let go," I promise, and I grip the ladder harder. For one second, I think I might have said, "I won't let *you* go," but I play the words back in my head and decide I didn't.

We develop a system over the next half-hour. Every few minutes, Jimmy climbs down, scooches the ladder a few inches to the right and climbs back up to paint the next bunch of curlicues and the here-and-there cherubs scattered across the roofline.

The rest of the guys zip up and down their ladders like Keystone Kops, slapping on paint.

P.J.'s going full throttle with his joke. "So dig, the guy's there a couple of weeks eating nothing but Shlemma Pie. Little by little he gets his strength back. Finally he figures he better get back to the wife and kids. He grabs an armload of Shlemma Pies and heads down the mountain. But it's all blizzardy so he gets completely lost. He's eaten his last pie when miraculously, he finds civilization! He hops a steamer for home and everything's cool for like a year. But then it starts nagging at him really bad. He can't seem to forget about Shlemma Pie."

I nod encouragingly…go on…go on…But what I'm really doing is holding the ladder for Jimmy. I look up and watch him dip his brush in the paint and wipe the excess on the rim of the can, and I think it might be the coolest little motion I've ever seen. He glances down at me and catches me staring up at him. I hope the look on my face isn't as dumb as I suspect. Rather than reconfigure my face, I just smile and he smiles back. I guess it's a version of what it must feel like to be boyfriend-and-girlfriend with somebody—a scenario that has always fallen into the way-more-trouble-than-it's-worth category in my opinion, but if it were like this, it might not be so onerous. (Thank you, Mindy, private SAT tutor, for that word.)

Sam steps back to admire his handiwork. "Not bad," he says.

"Not bad?!" says Jimmy, climbing down. "It's fan-fuckin'-tastic!"

He claps an arm around my shoulder and leads me into the middle of the street for a better view of the house. He ruffles the top of my hair. A big brotherly gesture. Or something else.

"Wait right here," I say and retrieve my camera where it's stashed by the front door. I'm so glad I have it. That settles it. Not selling the Leica. No matter what.

"Everybody on the porch," I say. The guys congregate, brushes and cans in hand, posing stiffly like the old man and woman in that painting where he's holding a pitchfork, and you can tell how hard their life is by the constipated looks on their faces. "American Gothic," I think. I'm about to tell them that's what they look like, but I'm not sure it's cool to know the name of a painting, even a famous one. So I keep my mouth shut and snap pictures. Click. Click. Click.

The guys move through a bunch of poses, goofing around, not taking the picture-taking very seriously, until Boo-Boo says, "Hey, man, we could get an album cover out of this."

"How about in front of the van?" I ask.

"Cool!" says P.J.

Sam says, "We better get Nina out here," and runs into the house.

On a whim (not a ride I usually take), I grab a paintbrush and swirl turquoise spirals around a rust spot on the door of the van. The guys join in, trailing their brushes along the van until all these organic patterns spread across the side as though the paint were an oil slick. Flowers with loopy stems, vines that curl back on themselves, amoebic designs—chevrons, bubbles, multi-eyed peacock feathers.

By the time Sam comes out of the house with Nina in tow, one whole side of the van is rocking the new paint job. Jimmy pulls Nina in front of the van. But she's not about to smile. Click. One shutter snap and she disappears back into the house. Fine by me. I've noticed that there are certain girls who shall remain nameless (in my class: Claire Warner and Amelia Sandrick) who positively grow porcupine quills when other girls are around. They like to be *the* girl in a group of guys. Even if they pretend it's because they are one of the guys, it's not. Nina must be one of those girls. Or else—and here comes a possible epiphany of the supremely stomach-wrenching variety—am I?

Fortuitously, the moment doesn't allow for introspection. Jimmy nods toward the van and says to me, "It was your idea, let's take her for a spin." He tosses me the keys. "You know how to drive, don't you?"

"Well…" I say, "I don't actually have my license. I mean, of course, I know how to drive. Who doesn't know how to drive? I've taken lessons and everything. I had this lunatic driving instructor—yada-yada-yada about his Italian wife all the time, as though I cared that Loretta made her own manicotti from scratch. So yes, of course, I know how to operate a motor vehicle. It's just that I have sort of a…shall we say… tenuous relationship with certain elements of the actual driving process…"

Jimmy shoves me into the driver's seat. "You know how to use a stick?"

"Now that's a loaded question," I say. I have absolutely no idea why. Jimmy looks at me strangely for a moment, a little wrinkle forming between his pinched eyebrows. And then I get it. It sounded like I was panning for sexual innuendo. The humiliating truth is, sex is such a theoretical topic for me—like string theory or non-Euclidean geometry—that I wouldn't even know where to find its facetious distant cousin, innuendo, if I had to.

I fumble with the keys like a total geek. They even slip out of my hand so that I have to grope for them under the seat. When I finally find them, I can't make the engine turn over. It sounds like it's clearing its throat, but doesn't quite make it until the fourth try. My conspicuous lack of automotive aptitude doesn't exactly inspire confidence among the guys. Suddenly, P.J. really needs to catch some z's; Boo-Boo has some drumheads in need of replacing; and Sam remembers that he promised to give Jennifer a foot rub. The guys wander back into the house one by one as Nina emerges, backpack in hand—my backpack. She tosses it into the van. "I know how badly you want to get home," she says.

"Thanks," I say.

Nina fixes her gaze on Jimmy. "You, get your ass back here in a hurry. We've got rehearsing to do."

"Yes, Mother," he says. I see the sting in Nina's eyes before she turns and heads back into the house.

Jimmy jumps into the passenger seat. "Left foot, clutch—right foot, gas."

"I can do that," I say, even though I don't believe it.

"Of course you can."

I've never driven a stick. I let out the clutch and press the gas. The engine revs, but the car doesn't go anywhere.

"You've got to put it in gear first," says Jimmy. "Straight up and to the left." I grab the stick and jerk it back and forth. Jimmy places his hand on top of mine and eases it into gear. It's tempting to give up and let him guide my hand the whole time, but gradually I get the hang of it—the rhythm of the clutch and gas in syncopation with steering. It's kind of like patting your head and rubbing your tummy at the same time. It requires laser concentration I have a hard time conjuring given that Jimmy keeps his hand poised over mine, hovering a mere inch or two above, just in case.

By the time he directs me to turn right on Oak, I'm feeling like I may actually be in control of this machine, enough so that I can take in the scene.

Young parents with scruffy children wave and flash peace signs at our psychedelicized van.

On one side of the street, a mime troupe paint one another's faces.

On the other, marchers gather, pumping their fists in the air as they shoulder flag-draped coffins down the sidewalk.

We get stuck behind a tour bus. A cluster of hippies alongside hold up giant mirrors to the passengers inside.

I turn left on Presidio. The entrance to the Golden Gate Bridge looms up ahead. "Oh, shit," I say.

"You can do it," Jimmy assures me. "It's a road like any other."

"No, it's not. It's a very high road with very low edges."

"You're perfectly safe."

I pull over to the curb and manage to jerk it into park. "There's no reason for me to cross it anyway," I say.

"I thought you wanted to go home."

I wipe my sweaty palms on my jeans. "I thought I did."

"Thought you did?"

I nod.

"And now?"

"I'm not so sure. I mean…"

"I mean, I mean, I mean," he says. "You're always saying that. Why don't you say what you mean in the first place?"

"I mean," I say in spite of myself. "That is to say, I don't think I'm quite ready to go home after all."

Suddenly, here in the car with Jimmy Westwood, home has lost its appeal. What does my regular life have to offer anyway? Sarah being annoyed with me for missing that party. My mom being annoyed with me for interfering with her social life. My dad being annoyed with me for commandeering his weekends. Why hurry back? As if I even know for sure how to get there.

"I like it here," I say.

My hand is still on the stick shift, Jimmy's hovering above. He lets his drop onto mine. "I like you, too," he says.

"That's not what I meant," I say. "I mean…"

And then Jimmy leans over and kisses me. *That's it*, I think, *my first kiss*. I always sort of thought that like so many wait-for-it things, it would end up being a giant less-than. But as it turns out, it isn't. I'm supposed to be immune to moments like this. Turns out I'm not.

"What was that?" I sputter. "I mean, I know what it was, of course. Obviously. But, out of morbid curiosity, was it a kiss to help me get over my little impending bridge episode, or was it intended to shut me up, or was it supposed to communicate some feeling of affection or possibly some other…"

He kisses me again, holds the moment a little longer. "That one," he says, "was definitely to shut you up."

He kisses me a third time. My brain goes into overdrive. Part of me wonders if I am going to do everything wrong. Part of me wants to remember every minute detail to tell Sarah. Part of me wants to burst out laughing that this is actually happening. But what I do is this: I close my eyes and I kiss him back.

CHAPTER

14

"WHY AM I not surprised?" says Nina when Jimmy and I appear back at the house. I don't even care that she's so rude. Her whole tough-guy persona doesn't scare me anymore; she has receded, like in those documentaries where the background shrinks into the distance so that the person the movie is about—the Nazi hunter or the anti-bio-engineered food crusader—stands out like a sort of paper doll 3-D cut-out.

"Whatever," says Nina. "Move your ass. The guys are setting up at Frizzie's. He's giving us a slot."

"Tonight?" asks Jimmy.

"Yup. And we have to make it great if we're going to be ready for the Fillmore."

❧

Frizzie's turns out to be a dingy coffee house, little more than a run-down room, movie theater dark, with a spit of a stage at one end. The voice coming from the stage is unmistakable: that sandpaper rasp.

When I can finally focus in the darkness, I see Royce on stage, making love to the microphone clutched in his hand, one foot planted firmly on the base of the mic stand as if to prevent the thing from swooning under his spell. He doesn't have a great singing voice, but it does have a quality that's kind of compelling: something threatening, even dangerous, though his voice is not exactly what he's selling.

I stand in the back of the room with Jimmy and the other guys, and Nina, too, listening as they talk to Frizzie, a gangly hippie with electrified hair. He's giving them the low-down, explaining that they will have to set up fast, right after Royce. He nods in my direction. "I didn't know you had two chicks in the band."

"She's not in the band," Nina snaps. She cuts through the tables toward the front where Royce is finishing his set. There's decent applause, enough so that when he leaps off the stage and struts past Jimmy, he says, "Follow that."

P.J. and Sam take the stage along with Nina. Boo-Boo positions himself behind the drums.

"Wish me luck," Jimmy says to me.

"Good luck. You're going to be great." He squeezes my hand in the dark, then kisses my forehead and bounds to the stage, leaving me alone in the back of the place, feeling strangely like half-a-something with him no longer at my side—a feeling that stomps all over the independence I've cultivated so painstakingly. But it also makes me feel more powerful, like it actually makes you stronger to feel connected to somebody else.

From the stage, Jimmy motions for me to sit up front. I weave through the tables, take a seat, and look up at him. If I saw some random girl sitting at some guy's feet with the look on her face that I feel taking over my face right now, I'd make fun of her. Plain and simple. I would turn to Sarah and say, "Look at that nitwit. I mean, get a life." But at this moment, I am *that girl*, which proves beyond a doubt that I have slipped through a crack in the time-space continuum so seriously major that it put all my personality traits on shuffle.

I'm sitting close enough to the stage that I can hear Boo-Boo say to Jimmy, "Dig it, a room full of living, breathing bipeds."

This is going to be different from their performances in the parlor. For one thing, they're going to have to make it through a song. Nina gives Jimmy the evil eye: if they're not ready, it's his fault.

"*It's No Secret*," says Jimmy.

Nina shakes her head no. That song's not ready.

He nods. Yes, it is.

Boo-Boo counts them down, drumstick against drumstick, and they break into the opening riff. Jimmy steps up to the mic.

"*It's no secret...How strong my love is for you.*" That first line sounds pretty okay.

He looks right at me when he sings, making it hard not to take the lyric personally. Boo-Boo drives the beat; P.J. manages a strong bass line; Sam plays solid lead guitar. They've got a folk-rock thing going that's very…sixties, oddly enough, but not old or clunky or too psychedelic. They're almost good.

People wander onto the postage stamp of a dancefloor. Bodies swaying, bobbing, surging. I almost feel like dancing, but I wouldn't dream of it, even though there are all imaginable configurations of singles, couples, clumps. I stay put, watching Jimmy… until Royce sits down at my table. Then I watch Royce out of the corner of my eye as he watches me watching Jimmy. Royce scoots his chair closer to mine. Jimmy strums a sour chord. Nina leans in to sing into Jimmy's mic. Her voice—powerful, yet unexpectedly tender—pulls Jimmy back to the melody. Their voices do something magical together; they make a third voice…or is it one voice?

But Jimmy's mistakes have already thrown the other guys. Sam comes in too soon. Boo-Boo blows his bit. P.J.'s harmony is sharp…or flat, I'm not sure. That judge on *American Idol* would call it "pitchy." The song sputters to a premature end. A hiccup of weak applause from a table in the back.

"That was a piece of shit," says Nina, loud enough that she doesn't care who hears.

Jimmy stays at the mic. "Okay, folks, we're going to kick in our spurs and try that again." He runs his fingers through that lock of hair that falls over his eye, brushing it back. It flops back as he looks down at his guitar, picks out the opening lick, nods to Boo-Boo. But Boo-Boo misses the cue and fumbles for the beat. They're a mess. I will them to do better—at least to make it through one song. But there's another impulse buried under that one, an impulse that fills me with guilt—and that's the impulse for them to bomb, to bomb really big, so that Nina will disappear from Jimmy's life. Poof. Not that I qualify as being in Jimmy's life, even as the tiniest bit player, but I want that girl gone. I could live with the guilt.

As if prompted by my psychic power, Nina grabs her carry-all—an oversized suede thing—and announces, "I'm outta here."

"We're just warming up," says Jimmy. "We can do this."

"Not tonight we can't." Nina jumps off the stage and makes a beeline for the door. Jimmy follows her through the darkness. "Nina…!"

The whole place is pin-drop silent. "We've been sitting around on our asses waiting for you," says Nina. "Well, I'm tired of waiting." She stops in her tracks and turns to face him.

"I thought you were here for the music," she says, "but all you want to do is chase little girls and play Sir Galahad." Disgusted, she flings her tambourine at the stage.

Royce intercepts it mid-air as Nina marches out. He presents the tambourine to me with a flourish. "Guess it's your turn now, Sunshine," he says.

My turn for what? To join the band? Or to replace Nina in some other way? Royce turns on the heels of his snakeskin boots and struts out of the club. After Nina? I'm so confused. All these players. All this drama. All that crap I used to make fun of.

Frizzie bolts to the stage. "All righty then. Moving right along…"

With that, Jimmy and the rest of the guys are summarily dismissed. I go with them.

◦⌇◦

"We're better off without her," Jimmy says to the guys as they trudge along, lugging their instruments. They exchange looks—who's he kidding? "We'll have a cleaner sound," he adds, trying to convince himself.

"Yeah," P.J. says, "who needs those great harmonies?"

"Don't get me wrong," Jimmy explains. "Nina's voice is great, but sometimes it's too pretty. We should go for a different sound."

"Yeah," P.J. can't help himself. "Who needs pretty?" Boo-Boo elbows him.

"You know what I mean," Jimmy elaborates. "We should go more rock, less folk. Like where Gracie's taking the Airplane."

"'Nuff said," says Sam.

Jimmy shoots his fist in the air. "We can do this!" he says. The guys raise their fists in solidarity, declaring themselves a band—even if no one is saying they're not quite as good a band as they were fifteen minutes ago. Before Nina walked out. Jimmy throws his arm around me, the tambourine in my hand jingle-jangling absently in time to the jingle-jangle of my jump-started heart.

15

THE GUYS gather in the parlor. It's a different house with Nina gone, less static electricity in the air. I sit on the couch, snapping photos in order not to feel like a total appendage. Even though it's late and they're licking the wounds of public humiliation, Jimmy wants to get right to work. Kind of ironic given that's what Nina was pushing for all along. But they still fumble—missed cues, off harmonies, the beat lost in the muddle of warring keys. They wrestle their way through the opening bars of a few songs, but grind to a halt every time.

"We're missing something," says Sam.

Nina is the white elephant in the room—her absence, so palpable it's like its own kind of presence, weighs more heavily than their failure to make it through a song.

"What we need," says Jimmy, "is our trusty tambourine." He looks at the tambourine where I have tossed it on the coffee table—an old steamer trunk plastered with stickers from some stranger's far-flung travels. Then he looks at me.

"I can't," I protest. "I have a certain difficulty distinguishing the downbeat from—what do you call it? One doesn't actually call it the upbeat, does one? What I'm trying to say is that I'm rhythmically challenged. Or impaired. That's an interesting distinction, don't you think? Which would be more apropos? I'm going with impaired. I am seriously impaired, rhythmically speaking. Which doesn't mean when I'm speaking, but you get the idea..."

"Just be quiet and shake the friggin' thing," says Jimmy.

I pick up the tambourine.

Feel A Whole Lot Better," says Jimmy. He counts down. It sounds vaguely familiar—an ancient oldie. But I have no clue what the tambourine is supposed to be doing. And, as I ventured to explain, I cannot rely on any innate ability to guide me. With Boo-Boo groping for the beat on the drums, I certainly cannot find the downbeat, the upbeat, any beat.

Once again, they give up. Song aborted. And then silence.

P.J. ventures, "Listen, Jimmy, I've been thinking... you know, man, before this whole Nina thing even went down, that maybe this isn't the groove for me."

"What?" asks Jimmy.

"You know," P.J. goes on. "I've been thinking about heading up north."

"Hang on," says Jimmy. "We're on the verge. I feel it." A tinge of panic in his voice. Normally that would make me want to say, "Man up." Instead, it makes me want to run over to him and wrap my arms around him and tell him that he's brimming with talent and promise, with vision and genius. It makes me want to tell him I believe in him.

P.J. continues. "No, man, I'm due at the draft board next week. I've got to get myself up north before I find myself knee deep in a rice paddy."

Jimmy nods. "Okay, man, you do what you gotta do."

P.J. clamps Jimmy in a bear hug and starts packing up his gear. Even though P.J., like the rest of these guys, is older than me, suddenly he looks so young. I can't picture him on the other side of the world, lugging a gun through *Apocalypse Now*. It makes no sense. It's enough to make a person thrust a clenched fist high in the air and join the chanting.

Jimmy offers Sam and Boo-Boo a wan smile. "Okay, guys, power trio!"

Sam looks down at the ground. "Dig it, Jimbo, I'm not sure I really belong here either."

Jimmy interrupts him, "Things are a little tricky right now. I get it…"

"I've got the baby coming…I gotta make some bread…," says Sam.

"Go," says Jimmy. "With our blessing. Right, Boo-Boo?"

"Don't look at me," says Boo-Boo. "I'm just the drummer."

"And that's why I can always count on you."

"Truth be told, bro, word is Deadly Nightshade lost their drummer and Gilbert and Tony have been asking around..."

Jimmy doesn't have anything left in him. "They're really good," he says, nodding to Boo-Boo. "You should go. It's a perfect gig. Shit, they'll be lucky to have you." Then he gets up from the moth-eaten sofa and walks out of the room.

I try not to let myself think about how I'm kind of the reason for the dissolution of this band.

CHAPTER
16

"IT'S MY fault," I say, sitting across from Jimmy at the kitchen table, a cracked glass slab balanced on a peeling brass base. "I've gone all Yoko Ono on you."

"Huh?"

"I've come between John and Paul and broken up the Beatles."

"What?!"

"I mean...you know...," I recalibrate quickly, but this is not an easy one. I'm in a world where the Beatles are still going full steam. "It's possible that the Beatles might break up some day. And it's possible that said break-up could be because some woman comes along and insinuates herself into what, I'm not going to lie, is arguably, not even arguable...no basis for argument whatsoever...the most staggeringly stupendous song-writing team, not to mention two-fourths, as in a full one-half of...again, there's no denying it...the musically, not to mention culturally, most significant group in the history of the world."

"Never," says Jimmy. "The Beatles will never break up. You're talking crazy again."

"Well, let's just suppose they did. And let's just suppose common lore held that it was because of a woman...I don't want to be the one who does that to your band. Not that I'm calling myself a woman... you know, I'm just a girl really, and the last thing I want to do is presume to think I could influence anything you might do personally or professionally... that is, if you think of music as your profession, or maybe it's more of an avocation, but you wouldn't say avocationally..."

Jimmy shakes his head. "We've been foolin' around off and on all year and it's never really come together."

"You know," I say, "for a minute there last night, at the club, you guys sounded almost..."

"Bearable?"

"No," I insist. "It was good. Actually, you reminded me of something I've heard before. I don't know, like on MTV maybe."

"I don't know that station."

"No, I guess you wouldn't." I switch gears. "You can't give up."

"Why not?"

"I don't know. But you just can't. I have this weird feeling. I know I've proven myself to be this sort of walking, talking conglomeration of nothing but weirdness since I've been here...not to mention now…as in, since I've been here *and now*…" Jimmy shakes his head. I tire people out. "But my point is, not that I haven't taken the polar route to get there… my point is, you can't stop. You cannot quit. You're meant to make music."

"I don't know…"

"That's who you are."

"What I'm meant to do right now…" says Jimmy, "is get some Sam Wo's."

ৎৡ৯

Thirty minutes later we're trekking down Grant Avenue in the heart of Chinatown. I haven't been there in ages, not even since my dad has been living in the city. And I've never been here at night. Even at this hour, the whole place buzzes with life; people bump into you with every other step and try to hustle you into this restaurant or that cheesy gift shop. Glistening whole ducks, shellac-shiny, hang from hooks in windows. The smell of deep fat blankets the street. At one point, a live fish flops from its bucket onto the sidewalk in front of my feet. I shriek and hop to the side, and Jimmy laughs.

We pause to study the celebrity photographs in a glassed-in case at Empress of China. I read the autographs, searching for a familiar name or face. Burt Reynolds and Zsa Zsa Gabor. Adam West and Faye Dunaway. Charo and John Wayne. Well, everyone knows John Wayne. (I happen to know him less from his "Howdy, pardner" movies than from my goofy philatelist period, circa third grade, that pretty much certified me as a card-carrying member of the nerd club.) We pass shop after shop, overflowing with merchandise, luring tourists to drop some cash on chopsticks fashioned from exotic woods or mandarin-collared sheaths in deep-sea turquoise and fire-cracker red.

Jimmy guides me onto Washington Street. "Here we are," he says, nodding toward a dilapidated storefront restaurant. Gold letters on the window: "Sam Wo." It's a skinny structure, not much wider than the door itself plus the single-brick strip on either side. It's more like a lean-to squeezed upright by the adjacent buildings. It hardly looks sturdy enough to support the iron balcony on the third floor. Above the name, it promises, "Chow Mein—Noodles—Soups—Fish—Salad."

"Not exactly fine fusion dining," I say.

Jimmy shrugs, as if to say "whatever that means"—he has given up trying to decode half the stuff I say.

"But it looks great," I try again. "I love chow mein." Honestly, I'm not sure I've ever had chow mein. My parents are more let's-go-for-sushi types, or used to be when the three of us were "let's-going" anywhere.

"Really," I reiterate, "I love chow mein!" Such a stupid thing to say, let alone twice, like in *Dirty Dancing*, when Baby says, "I carried a watermelon," and then she can't believe she actually said something so dumb to Patrick Swayze in his tight black pants and unbuttoned-down-to-there white shirt.

"You don't really come here for the food," Jimmy says. "Don't get me wrong. The food is great. But you come here for Edsel." He leads me through the mayhem of the ground floor kitchen—flames leaping from oversized burners, cleavers beheading the ducks that were hanging down the street, a cacophony of Chinese piercing the steamy air.

We climb a narrow flight and a half of stairs—creaky and steep—to the bare bones dining room. The place is packed. Chinese waiters dash everywhere, delivering dishes under pockmarked chrome domes, shouting at one another and at the customers, too.

Clearly, Edsel is the man in charge—moon-faced with a crew cut, a die-hard sneer, and a stained white apron. He spots Jimmy and starts busing a table, even though the diners are nowhere near finished. The woman protests, but the man silences her, shaking his head with disgust—not with Edsel, but with his date for not knowing the drill.

Edsel ushers us to sit —"Shut up and sit down!"—then turns his glare on a window table. "Hurry up! You order now!" he barks, poking one of the guys in the shoulder with a chopstick.

"Retarded fatso," Edsel says to Jimmy, nodding toward the poor guy. Which is kind of a pot-meet-kettle moment, because Edsel must weight two hundred pounds himself.

"Whoa!" I say. "Not exactly PC."

"What?" asks Jimmy.

"You know…PC…Pretty cool." I change the subject. "I've been trying to go veggie, not full-on vegan, though I do think the whole gluten-free thing people are starting to mumble about has been trumped up by an evil wheat-alternative cartel, but that's another story. Anyway, tonight I'll make an exception 'cause I do kind of lust after fried shrimp."

Edsel overhears. "Fried shrimp—rip-off. Expensive but not filling. I bring."

"He brings," echoes Jimmy.

"He brings?" I ask. I don't think so. I'm sort of a picky eater.

Jimmy widens his eyes really big: don't blow it.

"He brings," I agree. I study the house rules plastered on the table: "No Booze, No Jive, No Coffee, Milk, Soft Drinks, Fortune Cookies." I'm disappointed about the fortune cookies, I must admit, but the caricature of Edsel on the sign intimidates me enough to keep my mouth shut.

Edsel slides up a small door in the wall and leans into the open shaft, yelling our order. I think they call it a "dumbwaiter"—talk about PC. He yanks the menu out of the hands of a customer taking too long to decide. "What is this?" he snaps, "a library?"

Then he grabs a teapot and two cups, wipes them out with a dirty rag hanging from his belt, and pours us tea. He pulls up a chair and joins us.

"Tea good for you," he declares. "Good for everything. Clear the mind. Good for stomach. Good for cleaning tabletop." He nods to me. "Drink. You drink." I do as I'm told. The tea burns my tongue, but I take another sip. I get the idea. When Edsel says drink, you drink.

"Who is your friend, Jimmy" Edsel asks.

"This is Mari...Mari, this is Edsel."

Edsel gives me the once-over, long and slow and quite unnerving.

"Be nice," Jimmy admonishes him.

"What you mean? Edsel always nice." Jimmy stares the truth out of him. "All right, Edsel never nice. What you want? Nice waiter or good food?"

"Good food," I answer.

"Smart girl," Edsel nods. "How come you have such a smart girl?" he says to Jimmy,. "She can do much better than you."

Jimmy laughs. "I know."

Edsel leans across the table and whispers to me, "I kidding. Jimmy's a good guy. I know him a long time. I trust Jimmy."

"So do I," I say.

"Okay," Edsel turns to Jimmy. "What wrong?"

"Nothing's wrong. Everything's great."

Edsel wags a finger at him. "Don't try to fool Edsel. I know something wrong. You better tell me now or you might be sorry later. Edsel doesn't always have time to spend with customer." But he has time to keep his eye on all the customers. As one group gets up from their table, he admonishes them, "Small check, big tip!" He turns back to Jimmy, prods him with his chopstick.

"Okay," Jimmy gives in. "I've got no song. I've got no band. I've got no nothing."

"Okay, Mister Feeling-So-Sorry-For-Myself. I tell you what you got. You got talent. You got youth. You got smart girl. What more you need?"

"A band and a song?"

"What you think?" Edsel puts me on the spot.

"I think…I don't know…," I say. "I think sometimes it's good to eat something so hot and spicy it makes you cry, so all the tears can find a way out." I wait for Edsel to make fun of me.

"I told you," he says, tapping an index finger against his temple. "Smart girl."

It seems like Edsel's stamp of approval is worth something to Jimmy; I'm relieved to earn it. Edsel heads to the dumbwaiter to pick up our food. A hippie hails him on his way. "I didn't want any meat," the hippie says. Edsel reaches a pair of extra-long tongs across the guy to the heaping plate of chow mein in front of him. He clamps a piece of beef in the tongs. "You no want meat?" He extracts a chunk from the noodles. "I pick meat out." A trail of brown sauce dribbles along the way.

The guy blots the sauce splotched on his notebook, opens it, and scribbles something inside. Something

155

about this guy—and the notebook—makes me look more closely. I've seen that leatherwork before. And the guys' face. Or a version of that face. It's like looking at a police sketch in reverse—instead of projecting how a missing child might have aged, this face is a younger version of one that I know. And then it hits me. I've seen Mr. Chappell record attendance in that leather notebook hundreds of times. But it's going to be a really long time before anyone calls him Mister. This version of Chappell doesn't look like a guy destined to turn into a man who would try to make a point with an Incomplete. I guess people change. Now that I think of it, right this minute, I'm not so sure I'm someone who cares all that much about the Incomplete that non-meat-eating hippie is going to jot down in his leather notebook in forty years.

CHAPTER
17

"EDSEL LIKED you," Jimmy says as we stroll down the hill after dinner.

"I have a way with people who don't have a full command of the English language," I say.

"I can see where that would be an advantage for you."

"Gee, thanks."

"I'm kidding," he says. "I mean that may be true, but you have a way with perfectly competent English speakers, too, like, for example, me." He shakes his head. "Look at that. You've got me talking like you now."

"I never knew I was contagious," I say. "I'm so sorry."

"I'm not," he says. And then he takes me by the shoulders and kisses me. Right there on Grant Avenue, Chinatown, San Francisco, USA. When I open my eyes, it's like the night has taken a highlighter to the street, amping up the volume on the sputtering kaleidoscope of multi-colored neon.

"It's like a neon dream," I say.

"What?"

"Look at this. It's amazing. Like a neon dream."

"That's it!" Jimmy says. "That's it!"

❧

We get off the bus right in front of the Fillmore, and Jimmy leads me around to the back. He bursts into the office where a young secretary sits behind a desk. "I've got a name!" he says.

"All God's creatures have a name," the girl replies.

"For my band. Neon Dream. We're going to be called Neon Dream."

"I still think there might be a band with that name already," I say. I told him that on the bus, but he was too excited to pay attention. "It sounds awfully familiar."

"Never heard of them." He nods to the secretary. "Go ahead, write it down. Neon Dream." He turns to me. "Now all I need is a band."

"Post a notice on Craig's List, and you'll have a band in no time."

"Who's Craig?"

"You know, online…I mean, maybe we should put up some flyers?"

❧

"Don't you love that smell?" Jimmy says, breathing deep the stinging sharpness of copy machine fluid. "It's the smell of getting things done."

"Or the smell of brain cells dying," I suggest.

"Don't be crazy. They wouldn't be allowed to use it if it weren't safe."

The print offices for the *Oracle* stay open crazy late. It's some sort of newspaper, though they don't seem to be much interested in the news. They're running off a ditty by Allen Ginsburg whose giant poem "Howl" we read in English last year (actually, Honors English, which explains why we got special dispensation to read a poem about junkies). Timothy Leary of LSD fame smiles on the cover of this week's edition of the paper.

Meanwhile, we're cranking out flyers on what Jimmy calls the "ditto machine." The pages spin off the rotating drum, one after another: "Musicians Wanted for Rock Band."

We spend the rest of the night wandering the city. If this were a movie, some dumb song would play under a montage of us: strolling down Van Ness, taping flyers in the window of a music shop; hopping onto a cable car, passing them out to passengers; taping them to the notice board in front of the City Lights bookstore in North Beach; ushering in the dawn in Golden Gate Park.

The park is different at this eerie non-hour—kind of scary, populated by vacant-eyed homeless and bedraggled runaways, walking symbols of how hollow the whole peace and love thing is going to become in the future that belongs to me. I'm staggered, actually, by a sense of loss for what is, at this moment in time, peaking. I rest my head against Jimmy's shoulder. Zeitgeist dreams may be ephemeral, but this guy is real—more real than whatever may or may not be waiting on the other side of the bridge, more real than the scraps of what used to be my family, more real than Yale.

Jimmy hands the last flyer to a smudgy kid picking out *Mr. Tambourine Man* on his guitar, then plops down on a secluded patch on the side of a hill and settles onto the prickly grass. He pulls me down next to him. I want to nuzzle in as close as can be, but I literally do not know how. And I hate when people say literally when they actually mean figuratively. I mean literally; my body doesn't have the vocabulary. So I lie alongside him and reach over and hold his hand.

"The sky looks different here," I say. "You wouldn't think so, but it does. It looks bigger."

"Maybe your eyes are just open wider."

"I wish I could stay here," I say.

"Why not?" Jimmy asks.

"I don't know. Just a few days ago, all I ever thought about was getting to my future as quickly as possible. And now…"

"And now what?"

"And now I'm not so sure the future's all it's cracked up to be."

"Let the future take care of itself," Jimmy says.

I prop my head up on my hand and look at him. We've been up all night, and he's having a hard time keeping his eyes open. I don't mind when he gives in and his eyes finally close because then I can really study his face. His lashes are ridiculously long and there's a little dimple on the left side of his mouth even when he's not smiling. I love that it's always there and kind of lopsided.

He opens his eyes. "You know, all we have is right now. You and me and right now." He takes my face in his hands and kisses me. He tastes like Sleepytime tea—woodsy, sweet.

"Right now..." I repeat.

Jimmy beats me to it. "I know," he says. "Right now is highly overrated."

"No," I say. "Right now is the most wonderful thing. As in Wonder. Full."

❧

Exhausted, we navigate the San Francisco hills in silence as we head back to the house. The pre-dawn fog hangs thick and damp, but after a while, sunrise slashes a streak of gold through the haze. In these night/morning hours, the cable car bells ring out their language only intermittently, though the guttural rumble of the cables themselves hums always underground—constant, mechanical, yet somehow an organic undercurrent. As we approach the Haight, this driving sound becomes the backbeat of the music wafting in the air from every open window, no matter the hour.

Inside the house, we head upstairs. I find myself in that same single bed, chenille bedspread wadded at the foot, but now Jimmy is lying next to me. I would have thought my brain chatter would be in high gear. Instead, cerebral radio silence. I actually feel safe and even calm, unconcerned about all the things my mother told me made up a sort of a stupid checklist and why, if you couldn't tick them all off, you shouldn't rush into hooking up in the first place, and certainly not with just anyone. I rolled my eyes when my mom choked her way through the talk, but now I kind of get it. Jimmy Westwood is not just anyone. And surely leaping over decades qualifies as not rushing in, even if those decades wind backward. Who knows where I'll be when I wake up tomorrow? Wherever that is, whenever that is, there's no guarantee that Jimmy will be there, and checklist or no checklist, this moment in time—whatever time—is meant to be with him.

The tiny bells rattle as he pulls the gauzy top over my head. He smiles at their tinny clink, then kisses the little valley above my collarbone. Who knew that was such a magical spot? I close my eyes to help me do nothing but feel his lips there, and then on my neck— little kisses up my neck until he lands on my lips and I kiss him back and I'm so happy that I never kissed any other dumb guy before. This is who I was waiting for even if I didn't know it. The longer we kiss, the more

I feel like the rest of the world, like everything outside this room, this bed, is being sucked into a black hole and that we're the only two people spinning through the solar system. Not moon-and-June hyperbole—actual thought process, actual sensation.

And then I remember. "Jimmy," I whisper. "What about using something?"

"I've got it covered."

"And I think I'm supposed to ask you if…you know…what about AIDS?"

"AIDS?" he says. "Aids for what? Like toys or something?" He's lying kind of half on me, half next to me, and he props himself up on one elbow and looks at me. "Seriously?!" he says, incredulous.

"No! No, of course not like that. What would I know about that! Let alone having the nerve to say something…Eeeww! No. Just no."

"So, what? Do you need help with something?"

"No," I say. "No help." I kiss his eyelid. I kiss his other eyelid. "No nothing," I say. I kiss his lips. Again. And the future drifts farther away. I burrow my face into his neck and breathe deep. He is so warm—incandescent, I swear—and there's nothing to do but get as close to that heat and light as possible. When he touches me, I'm pretty sure the heat and light transfer to me. And the force field that usually zaps around me like an electrified fence to protect all boundaries fizzles away to stardust. And, for what feels like the first time in a very, very long time, I exhale.

CHAPTER
18

THE NEXT morning I open the front door to find a glazed-over hippie waving a flyer. "I'm here for the audition," he says. A trail of musicians carrying instruments and clutching flyers snakes behind him. It reminds me of that scene from *Mary Poppins* where all the nannies show up to be interviewed. Could one of these characters swoop in like Mary and turn out to be "perfectly perfect"? It feels like this whole band thing is in need of some spoonful-of-sugar swooping pretty desperately.

I usher the guy into the parlor. Jimmy lounges on the sofa, a sprawl of limbs. I can barely look at him without imagining myself tangled up in those limbs. He smiles at me like we have a secret, and I smile back. Actually, I'm already smiling. "Let's hear what you've got," he says to the hippie. The guy slaps on his guitar and sings a few bars of some song about a "plastic fantastic lover."

Over the next few hours, the candidates rotate through the parlor like they're on a turntable.

A kid no more than fifteen years old, sprouting a straggly first beard, rolls his flyer into a microphone and attempts his best Jim Morrison. *"Come on baby, light my fire..."*

A folkie type with a crewcut and a button-down shirt delivers an impassioned "If I Had a Hammer."

A pimply nerd with hornrims also thinks he can channel a little Jim Morrison. *"Come on baby, light my fire."*

A fat kid decorated in protest buttons strums his guitar and clangs the tambourine strapped between his knees. *"Like a complete unknown...Like a rolling stone."* He blows into his harmonica, sending spit flying.

A refugee from a Vegas lounge sidles up to me, crooning, *"Girl, you'll be a woman soon..."* Sleaze is clearly timeless.

An eager teenager in a tuxedo, no less, pulls a string of scarves from his sleeve and offers a bouncy "Do You Believe In Magic?"

Finally, a kid with a whopper Afro wearing a multi-colored dashiki ends the morning. Surprise, surprise: *"Come on baby, light my fire."*

It's early afternoon when I show the last candidate to the door. "That's the end," I say, returning to the parlor.

"You've got that right," Jimmy says. He is sitting on an amp with his head in his hands.

"We'll distribute more flyers later," I say.

"Why bother?"

"Because you have to," I say. "Because it's what you do. And because of the one heart at a time."

"I need my guys, but I blew it," Jimmy says. "Nothing's going to make them come back."

♧♤

Granted, I haven't been thinking much about getting home in the last day or so, but now I really back-burner the idea. A person can only come up with so many decent plans at any given moment—basically one. I can't stand seeing Jimmy this way. His misery is my misery. I want to be his hero. I've got to figure out a way to get the band back together.

First stop: Frizzie's. I leave Jimmy wallowing in his defeat and head to the club. Inside, the pitch dark blinds me. There's a weird rumbling sound punctuated by staccato bursts of air. Snoring.

"Hello?" I venture.

Nothing.

"Hello?" A little louder this time.

"Ten more minutes, Mom…" The voice, mid-dream fuzzy, comes from behind the bar. I peer over to find Frizzie asleep on a bare mattress. He manages to open one eye, struggles to focus.

"You're not my mom."

"Sorry. I didn't mean to wake you up."

"What time is it?" he asks.

"A little after one."

"In the afternoon?"

"Uh-huh."

"I've heard tell of one in the afternoon, but I didn't think people believed in it anymore." He performs a sort of jackknife to sit up and shakes his wild mane. "I remember you," he says. "You're the girl who came in with Jimmy."

He gets to his feet, switches on a light, and pours himself a cup of sludge from the bottom of yesterday's coffee. "So, what can I do for you?"

"I'm looking for some people," I say.

"Anybody in particular or do I get to choose?"

"The band. Jimmy's band. The guys all left, and I need to get them back."

"I have no idea where they are. No wait…I heard Nina's crashing in Sausalito and waiting tables at the Trident."

"Not Nina," I say, a little too fast and a little too adamantly. "I mean, I think Boo-Boo said something about some other band. Deadly Lampshade?"

"Deadly Nightshade," Frizzie says. "I did hear they lost their drummer. They used to practice in an old warehouse south of Market. On Mission maybe. Not sure if they still do."

❧

The neighborhood is seedy, to put it mildly. A couple of months ago, Sarah read about some uber-hip performance art event at a gallery around here and the two of us took BART into the city one Friday night to check it out. The neighborhood was completely different that night—a patchwork of lofts and sleek furniture show-rooms, funky little places to eat and chichi clubs. The kind of area my mother would pitch as "vibrant."

That night, Sarah and I sat on metal folding chairs and watched a six-foot woman wearing a black unitard stuff fistfuls of spaghetti into her mouth. She wore a miner's lamp strapped to her forehead. The crowd was rapt, truthfully, but Sarah and I had to bite the inside of our cheeks to keep from laughing.

Today, the lofts and showrooms, the restaurants and clubs, are nowhere to be found. Instead, I roam desolate block after block dotted with warehouses and slummy apartment buildings, half of them unoccupied except for the odd squatter. I walk quickly to be a moving target. On the fifth block, the buzzing distortion of electric guitars turned up to eleven rattles the windows of one of the warehouses. I crack the door and peek in.

Three guys with waist-length hair flail at their guitars, twirling their hair in unison. Boo-Boo sits behind them, pounding his drums mightily in order to be heard. He spots me in the shaft of light that streaks in from the outside world, stops playing and crosses to me. The other guys don't seem to notice; they keep slamming their guitars.

"What are you doing here?" Boo-Boo shouts to me.

"You've got to come back," I say.

"And leave these guys?" Boo-Boo says. "They're so…"

"Loud?"

"Yeah, well...at least they get it together to jam."

"Things are going to be different now," I say.

"Is Nina back?"

"Well, no, but Jimmy needs you." I take Boo-Boo by the hand and lead him outside so that I don't have to shout. Plus, that gives me a few moments to think of something persuasive. "He wouldn't want me telling you this," I say conspiratorially, "but Jimmy thinks you're the heart and soul of the band."

"Really?"

"Absolutely."

ॐ

I used to be a little freaked out by cable cars. They never seemed all that safe to me. And forget about when they're super crowded and you have to dangle from an outside pole. Even so, I leave Boo-Boo behind to pack up his drum kit, and take off on my own, grabbing the first cable car going in my direction. I'm still on a mission. Clanking along on some precarious conveyance is the least of my concerns.

Forty-five minutes and three cable cars later, I lift the heavy lion-headed knocker on the massive door of a Pacific Heights mansion. I can hear it echo inside when I let the thing fall with a metallic thud. A butler—black suit, the works—opens the door and appraises me coolly.

"I'm looking for Sam," I say.

"Master Samuel is in the basement," says Jeeves. Of course, I don't know if that's his name, but it should be. He leads me through the foyer with its high-gloss marble floor, then through a kitchen the size of an ice-skating rink. My mother would swoon. ("Fully appointed gourmet kitchen, a cook's dream come true.") He opens a door at the top of a flight of stairs. I head down.

The basement is Sam's territory all right. An entire wall is plastered with articles on conspiracy theories and photos of UFOs. Sam sits absorbed at his desk behind a model of Dealey Plaza and the infamous book depository, sliding a matchbox limo down the tiny street. I guess it hasn't been all that long since JFK's brains sprayed across that plaza, across the whole country if you want to wax metaphorical.

Jennifer is pulling a sheet of cookies from the oven in the mini kitchenette. She places it on the avocado-colored Formica counter. Her belly looks like it's gotten even huger—so much so that her belly button has popped out. It pokes against her tie-dyed T-shirt like the tied end of a balloon.

It's more than a little weird that a couple of hippies are living in this mansion with a manservant opening the door. I guess they've made their peace with the situation by confining themselves to the basement. I refrain from commenting, having more important things to accomplish than debating counterculture idealism versus the comforts of the bourgeoisie.

"Hi!" I say, startling them both.

"Mari!" says Jennifer. She's so happy to see me, though I don't really take it personally because the little I know of Jennifer is that she's generally happy to see people. She's a the-more-the-merrier type.

Sam lifts a hand in greeting, but is too preoccupied with the angle of trajectory out of the book depository window to turn around. I perch on the edge of his desk to get his attention.

"Sam," I say, "you've got to come back to the band."

"There's no more band."

"But there will be if you come back."

Sam looks up from his little toy car. I can see that he's made it limousine-sized by sawing one tiny car in half and gluing it to another whole one. "So Jimmy's sending you to do his dirty work, eh?"

"No, not at all. He doesn't even know I'm here."

He slides the sixth floor window closed and says, "I don't know…"

It seems like he's considering the possibility, so I decide not to say anything that may tip the scales the wrong way. Instead, I inhale the butter-brown sugar aroma. "Those smell really good."

Jennifer slides a spatula under one of the cookies, but it crumbles into pieces. "I don't know what I'm doing wrong," she says. Each time she tries to remove one from the sheet—more breakage. I nibble a handful of toasted oats and nuts—no longer a cookie, but crazy delicious. I take another handful. "Yummy anyway. Tastes like super good granola," I say.

"Like what?" Jennifer asks.

"You know. Granola." She's not getting it. "Like in a bowl. With milk."

I turn back to Sam, eyebrows raised, waiting for an answer.

"I don't know," he says, "we've got the baby coming. I probably shouldn't have a gig where I'm working nights."

"Your family will help," I offer. I mean, check out this house. A look flies between Sam and Jennifer. Maybe Sam's parents aren't the babysitting types. "What about ask Jeeves?" I say. "He seems like a great guy. Ready to pitch in at a moment's notice. I'd venture to say he's changed a diaper or two in his day. Nappies, he'd call them, being British and all. I'm assuming he's British. I hardly heard him speak. But maybe all butlers call them nappies…"

Sam gets up from his desk, scoops up a handful of cookie crumbles, and shoves them in his mouth. My pitch is not going well. He's considering his future. Seems like people in the past don't much worry about the future, but having a baby any minute must make the future seem way more like the present. Sam may not be wondering how he's going to send the little critter through private school, but he can't avoid thinking that feeding and clothing will be on his to-do list for the next eighteen years. Admittedly, making it as a musician is a long shot, but I suspect conspiracy theorist is even lower on the earnings food chain. Finally, I say, "You know, Sam, Jimmy thinks you're the heart and soul of the band."

He munches his mouthful. Then he nods knowingly, "'Nuff said." Jennifer smiles at me.

Sam's not much help in coming up with ideas about where to find P.J. All he knows is that there was some talk of his heading up north. "The draft," says Jennifer and a shudder runs through her as though the room were actually drafty.

"Probably taking the Greyhound," Sam guesses.

I grab another handful of cookie crumbles on my way out. "This is really good. Like majorly."

I'm getting pretty savvy at figuring out how to get around town. I hop on a cable car and head for the bus terminal, wondering why heading north would help a person avoid the draft. Oregon? Washington? What difference would that make? And then I remember our whole Vietnam War unit in Mrs. Wolper's AP US History. Duh. P.J. is headed for Canada.

It's late afternoon by now and the fog is rolling in off the bay. I'm hanging on to a pole on the outer edge of the cable car, and my mom's little flower child top is no match for the chill. The wind stings my face, bringing tears to my eyes. I have to transfer twice, and by the time I get to the bus station, I don't even mind that the place is so skuzzy. I'm just happy to be indoors where it's warm.

I scan the station for P.J., even though this place is a long shot. The molded plastic seats are tethered to each other and bolted to the floor as if someone might be overcome by the urge to grab one and make a quick getaway, like plastic chair heists are a thing. The faint smell of urine lurks under the odor of rancid french fry oil. In one corner, a couple of clean-cut college kids share an anemic-looking sandwich. A wino lies passed out across three chairs. A family monopolizes the middle of the room, the mom and dad arguing while the kids play War, that endless card game I used to play with my dad when I was little. I haven't thought of it in ages, but now, watching these kids, I realize my dad must have let me win. He must have wanted to make me happy. Or maybe he got really bored flipping cards and wanted the game to be over already.

I scan the room. Something is weird about the place beyond the sort of creepy dinge and grime. Then it hits me: not one person is on their laptop or their phone. No thumbs texting. And the craziest part is it took me a good three minutes to realize that's what's missing. I've turned so 1967!

I hear P.J. before I see him.

"So the guy's desperate for Shlemma Pie. He's got to get more. He puts himself in hock to get the bread for another expedition. Says good-bye to the family and heads back to the Himalayas. Finally, he's climbing back up the mountain. But wouldn't you know it? Another blizzard. All the Sherpas turn back, but not our guy. He's got to get that Shlemma Pie…"

I interrupt him. "You've got to come back to the band."

P.J. holds up an index finger—gimme a sec—then returns to the old lady's he's regaling with his joke. "Got to get that Shlemma Pie. Can't go on without it."

He turns to me. "What?" he says as though it's totally normal that I should show up there.

"Jimmy wants you back," I say.

"He doesn't really have the right…"

"I know."

"He wasn't really there for us," he says. "No offense."

I'm not sure why I would take offense. Or is he trying to say that Jimmy wasn't there for the band because of me? Okay, no offense taken. "Then come back for the music," I say.

"It's just music," P.J. says.

"Just music!" I surprise myself. "There's no such thing as just music. You ought to know that. You're from the sixties!"

"Huh?"

"I mean," I backpedal, "one of these days some middle-aged executive will make a fortune by clumping a bunch of prepubescent pretty boys together and calling them a boy band, but today—now—that's not what music is. Look around you! It's 1967! Music can change the world."

175

"You seriously believe that?" It's not that he doesn't believe it—it's that he's shocked I might. I momentarily consider a spiel about how he will be doing his part for humanity if he comes back to the band, but then it occurs to me. If he stays in the United States, does that mean he's going to be drafted? If I talk him into staying, am I offering up the band *and* Vietnam? I shove that notion way back in my brain because looking at P.J. right this minute, it doesn't seem possible that he could go off to war. Not possible.

So I say to him, "Listen, P.J., I know you've got a really good reason to leave, but Jimmy thinks you're the heart and soul of the band."

CHAPTER
19

THERE'S A TV in practically every room in my house and at least one of them is usually on. And yet, when I walk into the parlor and find Jimmy stretched out on the sofa flipping through channels, the television strikes me as an alien creature. So weird that I haven't missed it. Jimmy can't settle on anything to watch. "I Dream Of Jeannie"; "Batman"; some white knight riding his steed selling Ajax. "Stronger than dirt!" Jimmy keeps changing channels.

"Seven channels and nothing to watch," he says.

"How many?"

"Seven."

"As in one more than six and one less than eight?!"

He pauses on a commercial: a chic couple having fun with a vengeance—popping out from behind the columns in front of a tall building, smelling flowers, generally bouncing around the city with the kind of spring in their step that's supposed to prove they're having the best day ever. "When it's a turned-on time and a headache starts to turn you off, take Bufferin."

I let out a snort, can't help myself. But Jimmy doesn't laugh or even chuckle. He's too busy wallowing.

"What's up, Daddy-O?" Sam bops in like it's no big deal.

Jimmy sits up, his eyes wide.

Boo-Boo appears next, maneuvering his bass drum through the door.

P.J. is right behind him, guitar slung over his back. He rolls Boo-Boo's drum into the room like a hoop.

"What's happening?" Jimmy says.

The guys shrug and start setting up as Jimmy watches, confused. "What are you guys doing here?" he asks.

"We're a band, aren't we?" says Sam as he plugs into an amp.

"I don't know, are we?" says Jimmy.

"Of course you are," I say. "You're a great band!"

Jimmy turns to me. "Did you do this?"

"I did…But I couldn't have if everyone didn't want to be here, right?" I nod to them, hoping they'll pick up the cue.

"She's right, Jimmy," says P.J. "This is where we belong."

Jimmy says nothing for a long moment. I hope he's not going to get stuck on some crazy principle and wait for them to apologize for deserting him. That's how he still sees it, versus their believing he wasn't much of a fearless leader. The band's future—I don't know why, but I do believe they have one—is suspended over the gulf between the two sides, theirs and Jimmy's. I hold my breath to see who's going to be the one to take the leap.

Jimmy turns to me. "Is Nina coming?"

"I don't think so," I say. It's not technically a lie, but it sure feels like one. I really don't want to lie to Jimmy. But, more than that, I really don't want Nina here. I raise my camera to my eye to hide my face. It's ridiculous; even a white lie—kind of beige, actually—turns my face pink.

Jimmy straps on his guitar. "Okay," he says, "let's do this." As if returning to the scene of the crime, they start with "It's No Secret," the song that got them into trouble that night at the club. Boo-Boo counts them down, and they launch in. Having my face pressed up against the eyepiece of the camera lets me feel like I'm not just some groupie Velcroing herself to the band. Click. Click. Click. The sound of having a purpose.

The guys are almost not bad, getting better with each verse. I keep shooting, making a conscious effort to photograph not only Jimmy, but the other guys, too, though some sort of gravitational pull keeps tugging my lens back to him. Click.

Jimmy's face fills the frame: head bent forward over his guitar, eyes half-closed, lips slightly pursed in concentration. That might be a picture that could erase an Incomplete…if I still cared.

It's also the last shot on the roll. I figure they're going to be at this for hours, so I better restock. I wave the camera and mouth, "More film." Then I head out.

&‿&

The old camera store guy is sitting at the counter repairing a vintage Brownie—a boxy thing with a molded body and ridged sides. He looks up at me from under thick gray eyebrows sprouting a couple of errant feelers, which, in combination with the thick lenses of his eyeglasses, make him appear more Pixar insect than human. A *Wall Street Journal* lies open on the counter in front of him, a few stocks circled in red grease pencil. A three-legged tabby cat lazes in the corner behind the counter, disinterested.

"Hello, my friend," he says warmly. "Change your mind about selling the camera?" He nods toward the Leica around my neck.

"No, I just need a roll of film. And can you develop this one for me?" I plunk the finished roll on the counter.

"You want prints or a proof sheet?"

"Prints, I guess."

"Prints it is." He sings: "*Someday your prints will come…,*" and shakes his head at his own bad joke. "When do you need them?"

I look at the clock, a big round thing on the wall. It's nearly three.

"Four, four-thirty?"

"Today?" he asks, confused.

Oops. "No. Of course not. Not today. J.K. You know…just kidding."

"You young people," he mutters, "always in such a hurry. I usually hit the darkroom on Sundays, but I got nothin' doin' tonight, so I can have them for you tomorrow."

"Great. That'll be great," I say. "Thanks."

"Sure thing, my friend." He scribbles on a claim check and hands it to me.

"Don't you need my name?" I ask.

"I know who you are."

"You do?"

"Sure, you're the girl with the Leica. And I'm Vic." He extends his hand to shake. There's a hole in the sleeve of his cardigan.

"Nice to meet you, Vic."

"My pleasure. So, what'll it be?" he asks, running his finger along the bright orange boxes of film on the shelf behind him. "Black and white or color?"

"Black and white."

"A girl after my own heart. Black and white… nothing like it."

"That's funny," I say.

"What?"

"I thought in the sixties…I mean, you know, these days were all about everything being as colorful as possible."

"Maybe," he shrugs, "but I guess I'm not from these days. It happens. You wake up one day and time has passed you by."

"Tell me about it."

"In my day, I took pictures of the shadows. You can't capture shadow in color."

"You were a photographer?" I ask.

"Amateur city. But I won a few prizes here and there. Mostly there." He hands me the film. "Black and white it is."

I rummage in my backpack for some cash, as though more than the paltry $6.00 will have magically materialized. Vic raises a hand to stop me. "We'll settle up tomorrow," he says.

I look up from loading the new roll into my camera. "You sure?"

"Sure I'm sure."

Another customer enters the shop, ringing the bell over the door. The cat twitches in its sleep.

"See you tomorrow," I say, waving as I emerge onto Haight. Now I can't even think about getting home until after tomorrow; I have photos to wait for. Until tomorrow, here I am. I slip the new roll of film into my camera and snap it closed.

A girl wearing a flowing Indian-print skirt spins pirouettes down the sidewalk. Click. Frozen, gossamer, mid-twirl.

A hippie with hair bouncing down his back passes a homeless man, takes off his fleece-lined jacket and places it around the vagrant's shoulders. Click.

A cluster of kids—runaways, most likely—draw pictures on the sidewalk with chalk. Click.

A panhandler extends an open palm. "Spare change?"

"You know," I say, "you can get a Loveburger for a quarter," and I hand him one. He studies it in his hand. Click.

A radical plasters anti-war flyers on telephone poles. "Keep it up," I say to him. "The war will be over soon...I think...This one anyway." He flashes a peace sign. Click.

A girl about my age is weaving a tiny daisy into a crown of flowers. She places it on her head and tilts her face to the sun. Click.

She offers me a flower. I loop the daisy behind my ear as another hippie passing by places a string of beads around my neck. I rummage in my pocket for more change, but he holds up his hand to stop me. "They're love beads," he explains. "Love is free." Not according to Nina, I remember, but banish the thought of her.

I wander deeper into the Panhandle. Snatches of *Sgt. Pepper* drift from all directions on the heavily scented air—patchouli and musk. The Beatles sing, "*We hope you have enjoyed the show...*" Unable to help myself, I execute a twirl. One single, perfect pirouette.

A Greyline tour bus rounds the corner. The driver lifts a chunky microphone to his mouth and drones his patter: "Here in the Haight-Ashbury neighborhood, you will find the hippie in their natural habitat."

Tourists gawk from the safe interior of the bus. One Midwestern-looking matron shakes her head in disgust. Her sullen, teenaged daughter stares blankly out the window. But then, for a moment, we catch each other's eyes, the girl and I. I smile at her, and she manages a wan smile in return. I flash a peace sign. And...Click—a tourist at the back of the bus snaps a photo of me—a hippie, apparently in my natural habitat.

CHAPTER

20

"HASN'T THIS been the most fantastic day?" I say as I bound into the parlor. Evidently not. Not in this house. The fizz has flattened. Boo-Boo, Sam, and P.J. lounge on the sofa staring at each other. Jimmy is nowhere to be seen.

"You might want to steer clear of the boy wonder," Boo-Boo says.

"Yeah. Danger," says Sam. "Genius at work."

It can't be that bad. Undeterred, I head upstairs.

Jimmy is slumped, deflated in the easy chair where he sat the other night lullabying me to sleep. I sit on the bed, but he doesn't even acknowledge my being there. He's fiddling with the same melody that poured out of him then. It's not coming so easily now. He plays the same phrase over and over, trying different tempos, slightly different progressions, but the tune stutters along.

"You want to play it for me from the beginning?" I suggest.

"Everything I write is shit."

"So…," I say. "Want to play some of that shit for me?"

Nothing. Zippo.

"Not funny?" I say. "There's a rumor going around that you wrote an amazing song…"

"That was a long time ago."

"Nina said you had a broken heart." I hadn't really intended to bring her into this, but desperate times require desperate measures. (My mom uses that expression all the time, though I often question her definition of desperate times…and measures for that matter. For example, desperate time: running out of shaving cream in the shower. Desperate measure: using conditioner to shave her legs instead.)

"Nina said that?" Suddenly, he's interested.

"Yes."

"Yeah, well, she ought to know."

And then it hits me. All at once. Smack. How could I have been so dense? "It was her," I say, "wasn't it." A statement, not a question.

He says nothing.

"Well, isn't that just an a-ha moment as Oprah would say."

"Oprah?" he asks.

"You're so lucky to live in an Oprah-free world." I spit it out: "She was the one."

"Oprah was the one? Who's Oprah?"

"No," I say. "Nina. Nina was the one."

"The one what?"

186

"The one who broke your heart. It was Nina. Of course it was."

"So what?" says Jimmy nonchalantly. "She walked out on me a couple of years ago. That's what Nina does. She walks out. This time it happened to be from the band. And this time it's for good."

"She broke your heart and then you wrote the great song…" I'm thinking out loud, trying to connect the dots.

He says nothing..

"She's still in love with you," I say before I can stop myself. And once I say it, there's no dog-paddling back to the land of denial. "No matter what she says, she's still in love with you. 'The lady doth protest too much,' as old Billy Shakespeare would say…actually said…by which one means 'wrote,' not 'said'…But putting the bard aside, that's why she left. Not because you sucked at Frizzie's, but because she loves you too much to be around you without you two being… you know…being you two, like you used to be. Like she's always wanted it to be. She kept denying it, and I kept believing her. Because I wanted to. So badly. No wonder she hates me…I mean, not that you and I are anything. We're not, right? Anything?" I want so desperately for him to tell me I'm wrong that I cannot even look at him.

"You're crazy," he says, but he's not smiling. He's not kidding me. He doesn't want to hear any more about Nina. "Crazy," he says again.

"For thinking we might be something? I'm saying the opposite of that. I'm saying we're nothing. A big, giant, humongous black hole of nothingness."

Jimmy looks like I slapped him. "No, we're something," he says, "because you're not like anyone I've ever met."

"There are reasons for that," I say.

"I don't care about the reasons. It's true."

"Just because I'm different doesn't mean..." I can't finish. I can't come right out and ask him if he loves me. Because I know Jimmy is not someone who would lie about that. "I know I'm right. It's abundantly clear. 'Clear as an unmuddied lake' to quote *A Clockwork Orange*. Great book, better movie. Have you seen it? Oh no...probably not. But you should. Remember that—*A Clockwork Orange*. It's a personal favorite which probably doesn't say much for the resounding state of my psychological health, on which you have so astutely cast aspersions, but a brilliant movie is a brilliant movie regardless of the, shall we say, disturbing subject matter: the old ultra-violence as Alex would call it...He's the protagonist..."

"Not now, okay?" says Jimmy, neither charmed nor delighted, not even bemused, just disappointed and hurting. "I thought this band had a future," he says. "I thought I had a future with them. But I can't write anymore...So I love you...but stop. Just stop. Not now, okay?"

"What did you say?"

"I said I can't take that stream of consciousness thing right now."

"No, before that."

"I said I love you."

I love you, too! That's what I scream in my head. But, for once, I stop the words from tumbling out. Jimmy gets stupid when he's in love. That's what Nina told me, that his muse hangs out in heartbreak. Am I going to have to break his heart to make him happy? That makes no sense, but I can't think of what else to do. I'm not exactly used to putting other people's needs before my own, I admit it, but somehow allowing Jimmy to get this song out has become my need, too. If Jimmy needs a broken heart, I need a broken heart. I need to break both our hearts in one fell swoop. Who ever knew that love is such a crazy maze—a maze of need and sacrifice and pain, so that the minute you think you've found your way, you make a left turn, so unexpected and so sharp, it takes your breath away?

Words muddle in my brain. What do I say to him?

Let's be adult about it...we hooked up and everything, but...

I think we could be really great friends...

I'm really just passing through.

I wonder: am I passing through? What if I'm stuck here? I don't think I could handle 1967 without Jimmy. I know I wouldn't want to. But I know how much the music means to him, not even so much because of the Fillmore contract thing, but because of the look on his face when he picks up his guitar and starts to play. In spite of every impulse, I look him in the eye and say, "Well, I don't love you."

"You don't mean that," says Jimmy. "You never mean what you say."

"It's exactly what I mean," I say, and my cheeks turn hot. "You taught me that. To say what I mean."

"Then I guess you should go," Jimmy says.

I get up from the bed and cross to the door. I have to walk right by him, no avoiding it, and when I do, he grabs my wrist to stop me, but he doesn't look at me. He just holds me there for a moment and then lets go. And I keep heading out the door while he crumples up the piece of paper scrawled with his latest attempts at a song. He tosses it in the direction of the wastebasket where it joins a pile of wadded pages. Seems he can't even make a stupid basket. But I walk out the door anyway, like I couldn't care less. When, in fact, I care more than I've ever cared about anything in my entire life.

I grab a sweater hanging on the hall tree by the front door and bundle it around me against the bone-chilling cold that comes with sundown in San Francisco, even in June. I hit the sidewalk and glance up at Jimmy's window, but my vision is too blurred by tears to see. I wish I were home, even if that means being at that lame-ass, beer-sloppy party with Sarah begging me to stay ten more minutes. Or would that have been yesterday?

I'm used to being alone. I'm certainly used to feeling alone even when I'm not. It's a major part of my self-construct—my ability to be alone and be just fine, thank you very much. Kind of a badge of honor. But as I head down the street, a sense of profound aloneness sucker punches me—the kind of emptiness that drops into your body like a lead weight only in the sudden absence of something else, something that was there a mere moment ago. It's the alone—bitter and crushing—that drowns you when something, someone, suddenly goes. Disappears. Vanishes. When my father moved out, I promised myself I would never feel that way again, but now here it is, fist to solar plexus.

And the worst part is that it would be so easy to fix. Walking back into that house and being in the same room with Jimmy would fix it. He wouldn't even have to touch me, and yet, I can't stop thinking about him touching me.

After a few blocks, I find myself in front of the Loveburger joint. Inside, the little boy behind the counter slides a patty onto a bun and places the finished product between a guy and a girl huddled together under a single parka. The girl brushes aside the matted fur collar of the grungy jacket where its sharp, petrified clumps poke at her cheek. The guy dabs the ketchup dribbling down her chin, then licks the last of it away, his tongue tracing the path to her mouth. I look away, not out of disdain, but because of a wild ache deep in my chest. A longing I cannot name.

From the sidewalk, I study the sign in the window—handmade, as if by kindergartners. Loveburger twenty-five cents. Suddenly, the counter boy appears at my side. He deposits a hamburger into my hand. It's unwrapped, but fresh and hot. "Here," he says. "Eat this."

"But…" I stammer. And then I burst into tears.

"It's okay," he says, patting me on the arm, "the twenty-five cents is optional." The little boy smiles at me, then heads back into the diner. I wonder who that little boy will grow up to be, has grown up to be. Whoever that may be, I hope—wish-upon-a-star hope—that he remembers the little boy who gave a hamburger to a girl who looked sad.

CHAPTER
21

"WHERE YOU headed, Sunshine?" Royce's voice, all smoke and rasp. He pulls up beside me in his Mustang, top down. The wind blows his hair away from his face so that I am struck by the plane of his cheekbone angling down to a chiseled jaw. It would make a great photo, but I'm not about to take his picture.

"Where you headed?" he tries again, as if I didn't hear him the first time.

"Nowhere."

"Get in," he says, "it so happens I know how to get there."

I don't get into the car.

"C'mon, we're going to a party."

"Parties are against my religion," I say. My fallback line.

"Not tonight. Tonight you're an atheist." I can't help but crack a smile. "Gotcha," he says, and he leans across the front seat and throws open the passenger door. Maybe it's because he made me smile in spite of myself. Maybe it's because I want to prove to myself that Jimmy's not the only guy on the planet. Maybe it's because it's really cold standing here on the sidewalk. Maybe it's because I don't give a shit about being safe at this moment. Whatever the reason, I get into Royce's car.

"So how are things at the house?" Royce asks.

"I don't know."

"Oh, you know. And you know that I know that you know." His voice softens as much as it can. "You can trust me."

"I rather doubt that," I say. "Besides, it's not my nature."

"Yeah, well...neither were parties." He turns up the radio full blast and sings along. "*Don't you want somebody to love / Don't you need somebody to love / Wouldn't you love somebody to love...*" He stops singing. "So, Nina split."

"Seems like it," I say.

"And I'm guessing you don't mind that so much."

"It's none of my business."

"Whatever you say, Sunshine. But I swung over to Sausalito last night, and she happened to be my waitress at the Trident, so I'd say she's not diggin' the band scene so much right now." He stops at a red light, nods to the driver of the car next to him—a wild-haired girl driving a Porsche Sunbeam convertible with a God's-eye painted on the door, like the ones Jennifer makes with yarn. She smiles back from behind her rose-tinted wire rims and chugs something straight from the bottle. "Cold Duck," it says on the label.

"She's drinking and driving right there in the car," I say. "That's against the law."

"Tell Janis that." On cue, the girl blows Royce a kiss. "Janis does what Janis likes," he says.

"Janis?!"

"Yeah."

"Janis Joplin?" I say.

"Yeah, you know her?"

"Janis Joplin?" I repeat, incredulous. "Janis. Joplin." The light turns green, and she screeches off, leaving me to wonder how much longer she has before she self-destructs. Another one destined to bite the dust.

As Royce turns onto Fulton Street, there's no mistaking that the party house is up ahead. A real true mansion, the biggest on the block. It seems like the mass of green across the street—all of Golden Gate Park—serves as nothing more than the personal front yard for this house. Swarms of people move toward it, like lemmings, from all directions, mingling on the steps out front, crowding past the columns and across the wraparound porch to head inside. The circus has come to town and staked its claim right here on Fulton.

Inside, the haze of weed takes my breath away. I smoked with Sarah a couple of times, chiefly to be able to say we had—not that anyone was asking—but we agreed it wasn't much fun. I hated the burn in the back of my throat and how it made me feel wobbly.

Mostly, I hated the way it made me lose track of time. I found that very disconcerting, because if there's one thing I pride myself on, it's my perception of time. Most mornings I wake up seconds before my alarm, and I always know when the bell is going to ring at the end of class. Weed threw off my impeccable circadian rhythm, and that's too high a price to pay for a few giggles about stuff that wasn't even funny and the urge to eat every cracker in the house.

A few deep breaths, and I can feel the wobbles coming on. Add a whirling liquid light show and the whole planet starts to spin off course. Royce leads me from the foyer to what must be the living room, but it's more the size of a ballroom. A rainbow kaleidoscope pulses in time to the music, swirling across rosewood paneling and a massive carved fireplace. In the corner, a guy wearing nothing but American flag jockeys is painting Day-Glo swirls on the body of a naked girl. Fluorescent orange and carnation pink spiral up her thigh. In the opposite corner, a knot of hippies lounge beneath a swag of Indian bedspread and pass a hookah.

As a flashing strobe light takes over for the vibrating colors, Royce pulls me into the clump of dancers. Sounds like The Doors. Like Janis, Jim Morrison's not going to be around much longer. Crazoid that forty years later, I know these people as though they were old friends: Jimi Hendrix and Janis and Jim. Jimmy, my Jimmy, is right after all: music changes the world. At least a little bit. Because the music lives.

Gradually, all the dancing bodies slither to the floor. Royce pulls me down, too, and suddenly his hands are moving all over me...and more hands...too many hands...strange hands...other people's hands. I struggle to catch my breath under the acrid odor of weed and sweat, my breathing already skittery. Desperate to untangle myself from the human spiderweb, I wriggle my way free and swim upstream against the crowd, as the blinking strobe illuminates clothes flying off, one piece after another, in herky-jerky motion. I glance back only once. I'm not sure Royce even knows I'm gone—too many legs and arms, so much slippery skin.

I move out of the ballroom, but can't escape the crush. I can't fight being herded into a giant plastic thing, a structure of some kind. The plastic smells familiar; I'm not sure from where—chemistry class maybe, or like packaging. Polyethylene, I think. The doorway to what might be the dining room has been lined with a king-sized Hefty bag with a flap cut into the plastic as a door. Brobdingnagian. I move deeper into the amorphous plastic environment and the space gets darker and darker until, within moments, I find myself groping through pitch blackness. I cannot see my hand in front of my face. I feel only the press of bodies—many of them naked—and the claustrophobic choke of heat. Racing heart. Sweat gushes from every pore. Sporadic blasts of cold air prick my nostrils and chill the perspiration, freezing it against my skin. The cold must go with the constant whirr—a drone of white noise—some sort of industrial fan keeping the giant baggie inflated. All someone has to do is trip over the cord, jerk it from its socket, and the thing will deflate. Suffocation. Tomorrow's headline: One hundred hippies dead in humongous Ziploc—human sandwich gone bad.

Here in the pitch blackness, I wonder what my parents are thinking right this minute? Do they even know I'm gone or is this all happening in a time warp split second? Will it take forty years for them to know I'm missing? If they do know I'm gone right this minute in time, do they miss me? How could they not? And yet, why would they? Am I, my actual self, someone to be missed or do you automatically miss your child, like it's programmed into your parenting DNA? I crawl through the darkness, counting my breaths to make sure they don't stop, while the air weighs heavy and damp, and wonder how long it would take my parents to get over it if I never make it home. Am I going to die in a room-sized baggie in Haight-Ashbury in 1967?

The crunch of bodies grows denser like the plastic is shrinking in on itself. Knees and elbows poke at me. I crawl over hurdles of outstretched limbs interlocking in mystifying Origami combinations. I bump into something—a bottle—topple it and feel the spill, slick and unctuous, some kind of oil. It soaks into the hem of my blouse. I jerk my arm out of the stuff and set the tiny bells on the sleeves tinkling. It has the almost-no-smell of vegetable oil. I can only imagine how and where this oil is being slathered.

I keep crawling, as if moving without moving in a nightmare. The air takes on more weight. It presses on me from all directions, but I cannot manage to fill my lungs. I feel consciousness slipping away, but I move in the direction I came from, or think I came from. There is no such thing as direction in this blackness. I talk to myself in my head—*go on, go on, go on*. And then I can't go any further. I bump into something head-on. Someone. He grabs me by the shoulder. "No!" I shout, but it's just another sound under the music and the voices. I push the arm away.

"It's me." The voice—an unmistakable rasp.

"Get me out of here," I say, and I feel for his hand. "C'mon."

We crawl through the maze of bodies back, eventually, toward a streak of light, then finally through the portal. The ballroom, suddenly a haven of light and air, seems to have expanded in comparison to the confines of the plastic bag. I breathe deep, even though the air is noxiously sweet with weed.

"Heavy? Eh, Sunshine?"

I slump onto a random mattress and close my eyes against the too muchness of everything. "Total heaviosity," I say. "Never a goal of mine."

"You're pretty clear about things that aren't your thing."

I usually am. At least I used to be. "I like to have a plan for the future," I say, not letting on that at this particular moment, I have no idea which future I'm talking about.

"The future can always be rewritten," says Royce, and then he kisses me. Wet, choking, hard. Nothing soft or inviting. Nothing I want to yield to. Nothing like Jimmy.

I break away. "You," I say, "are not my future. Make no mistake. You will never be my future."

CHAPTER
22

"YOU OKAY?" A voice rouses me from a kind of stupor. I'm leaning against a storefront, my head tilted back against the plate glass. I'm sure I could remember how to open my eyes if I could only get my brain to communicate with my eyelids. I've never been so tired. "You okay, honey?" the voice asks again.

Finally, I open my eyes, though they do this weird fluttery thing on the way. The first thing I see is a frayed patch of gray yarn with a hole in the middle. The sweater worn by the old camera store guy. I raise my eyes to his face where he stands over me.

"Are you sick?" he asks. It's him all right, the old Pixar character.

"I don't know. I don't think so."

"You take something?"

"I don't think so," I say again. "I'm a little dizzy, that's all." Maybe I did take something that I can't remember. That's totally possible. I know you're not supposed to put down your drink at a party and then come back to it, not that I've ever had occasion to put that practice into...well, practice. I rifle through brain files for a test to run to make sure my faculties are still intact, but all I can come up with is counting backward by sevens. One hundred...ninety-three... eighty-six...I can't keep going, but I convince myself fatigue is the culprit, not my brain on drugs.

"Let's get you something to eat."

"I'm not hungry," I say. "I just sat down for a minute. I was at this crazy party, and I had to get out of there. I sat down for a minute to catch my breath, and I guess I fell asleep."

"I'll walk you home so you can get some good sleep," says the old guy. I think he said his name was Vic.

"I've got nowhere to go. I kind of broke up with this guy...if you can break something up that's not really put together, at least in any official capacity... you know, not with real emotional cement, sort of with old Scotch tape..."

"Let me fix you a nice cup of tea," says Vic. My first reaction is to say no. Why would I go home with this old coot? But then I think I could outrun him if I needed to, and I am super cold and a cup of tea sounds really good.

We head down Ashbury, and I'm pretty sure the old guy's okay. He's clearly a neighborhood fixture, raising his hand in greeting to nearly everyone we pass. "That's me," he says, pointing to a series of bay windows scalloping the sky above the record store.

I follow him around the side of the building, up a rickety flight of stairs.

"I leave the back door open," he says. "Truth is, I leave the front door open, too." Good to know, though I feel safe with this old man and really don't think escape routes are going to be necessary.

The door at the top of the stairs is peeling in patches, splintered in others. It opens into the kitchen. The room is a lot like Vic himself—untidy but comfortable. The countertop is cluttered with a haphazard collection of cookie jars—an owl wearing spectacles, a rotund piglet, a politically incorrect Aunt Jemima, to name a few. Stained coffee mugs and sticky silverware are scattered across the rest of the counter. There's a pot on the stove with the pasty remnants of what appears to be bean soup. Yup, the open Campbell's can—Bean With Bacon—sits next to the burner, a wooden spoon sticking out. It takes Vic a moment for the mess to register. "I wasn't planning on guests."

"Oh, that's okay. You don't have to think of me as a guest."

"I'm not much of a housekeeper," he says. "It's hard to remember to keep things nice when you live alone. No reason to, but I should anyway. It's been a while. Sometimes it feels like yesterday that this was a home, and we were a family living here. Sometimes forever."

"I get it," I say. "It feels like yesterday and forever since I've been home, too. But the funny part is, it may actually be." When I think about it, I have no way of knowing how long I've been gone. If you can travel through time, who knows what happens to the time you're traveling through. It could shrink or expand. Physics must dictate certain parameters, but there was no "time travel" unit in AP Physics that I can recall. I suspect there's some parallel between moving between two points in space and moving between two points in time. That much I remember: physics relies heavily on the relationship between time and space. Beyond that, I'm going with an all-bets-are-off situation. I like to think maybe I've only been gone a few minutes, for my mother's sake.

Vic puts the kettle on, washes out a mug, and dries it with a dishtowel embroidered with the saying, "There's no place like home."

"I don't know what I'm talking about," I say. "Time. It's bizarre." I look around the kitchen. "You should get a microwave. It would make life so much easier for you."

"I've heard about those cockamamie things. Too expensive. They'll never catch on when you can have a perfectly good stove."

I smile, let it go at that. The kettle whistles. Vic takes a teabag from the Lipton box, places it in the clean mug and pours the boiling water, dunking the bag vigorously. "There you go," he says, handing it over.

"Thank you."

"You are very welcome." He takes a deep breath. A little like right before Mr. Chappell told me about my Incomplete. "Your parents know where you are?"

"To tell you the truth," I say. "I'm not sure." I think about my mother. She must be really mad at me for going all melodramatic and disappearing. I wonder if she thinks I've been kidnapped or something, in which case she'd be so upset that our last conversation was a fight. I am.

We move into the living room. You can tell an old person lives here, not because he doesn't do the best job of cleaning up—which he doesn't—but because there's all this stuff around—a misshapen clay ashtray made by a preschooler, a pillow with initials needlepointed to form a crest, a bunch of purple glass grapes—little pieces of a life that look like junk to an outsider but must mean something to him or did once. What makes the room cool are all the black and white photographs hanging on the walls: buildings, the park, faces.

"Wow," I say.

"I used to know my way around a camera," he says. "Not so much these days. Kind of lost my…what do you kids say?…my groove."

I walk around the room, checking out each photograph. I pause at one in particular—a photo of a little boy, a toddler, head thrown back in laughter. "Did you take all these?"

"Guilty," he says, tossing some newspapers from the couch to the coffee table and motioning for me to have a seat. I sink into the sofa, lemon yellow with white windowpane checks, a remnant from a cheerier life.

"Poor old thing's a little lumpy," Vic apologizes. "Seen better days."

I hold the mug under my face. The steam washes away the stink of the party lingering in my nostrils. The cat from the shop downstairs wanders in like she owns the place, sort of cantering on her three legs.

"That's Tripod," says Vic.

"Great name," I say.

"She earned it as you can see." He pauses. "Maybe you should give your folks a call."

"It's not that easy." I blow on my tea and take a sip.

"Nothing worth doing is easy."

"It's hard to explain."

"Try me."

I'm too exhausted to come up with a reason not to tell the truth. "I'm from the future," I say.

"So your folks don't understand you 'cause they're from the past. Well, I'm from the past and you and me, we seem to be getting along hunky-dory."

"You don't get it."

"I do actually," says Vic. "I've got a son."

"It's complicated."

"From where you sit, it's complicated. From where I sit..." Vic's eyes dart to the photo of the toddler. "From where I sit, it's pretty simple. Who's right and who's wrong...that doesn't really matter much in the long run."

He misinterpreted me, of course—why wouldn't he? Why would he take me literally? You'd have to be crazy to believe someone was from the future. I consider trying again, but how can I convince someone else when I'm not convinced myself?

"My parents...," I say, but I don't know how to finish my thought. They what? They argue about who's going to get me every weekend like I'm the third grade hamster over spring break? Or, that cliché of clichés, they don't understand me? What's so special about that? It's in every teenager's job description to be misunderstood.

"That you're there for the people who mean something to you, whether they know it or not... that's all that matters." Says Vic.

I look over Vic's shoulder at that toddler laughing on the wall.

"That's my boy," he says. "When he was little."

"Where is he now?"

"He's in college. Studying computers of all things. Don't know what the devil he's going to do with that, but he thinks it's the way of the future. Can't persuade him otherwise. I guess when his mom and me split up, he sort of decided it was a lot less messy to spend your time with machines."

"My parents are divorced, too." My voice cracks a little. The cat jumps onto the couch, sidles up to me.

"She likes you," says Vic. "That's unusual." Doesn't seem like he's the kind of old guy who has a lot of guests for Tripod to like or dislike, but he also doesn't seem like the kind of guy who would say something just to be nice.

"It happens," he says. "Divorce. Never easy though. My wife, all of a sudden, after who knows how many years of marriage, she decides she wants to find herself. So she takes our boy and moves to a commune in the middle of nowhere." Vic clears his throat. "Then what do you suppose she does a few months later? She marries a banker. And where should she find herself but in a fancy apartment on Nob Hill. Very hoity-toity." He chuckles. "Life," he says, "go figure."

"That's funny, "I say. "My dad spent some time in a commune when he was a kid. I guess it wasn't... I mean, I guess these days it's not so uncommon. Excuse the pun. Bad pun, I might add."

"No excuses necessary. In my opinion, puns are the highest form of humor."

"My opinion, too!" I say. "So how often do you see your son?"

"Not much. He thinks I'm stuck in the dark ages."

"More like the darkroom ages," I say, raising a brow for effect. Not so sure about that one. Vic rocks his hand back and forth: so-so. "It won't stay that way forever," I say.

"Hope not."

"Someday..."

"Sure thing," says Vic. "There's always someday."

I wander over to the mantle. A photograph—just a snapshot, really—is stuck in the corner of a larger framed photo. I remove it from where it's slipped into the tarnished silver frame. It's the same boy as the laughing toddler, but older here, probably twelve or thirteen, and strangely familiar. He looks a lot like a boy I've seen somewhere before. Not in person, maybe. Maybe he was a kid actor. But it's more like I've seen him in a dream. Or in another photograph.

I turn to Vic, about to ask about the boy and how I might know him...but then I don't have to. Like in an old movie, everything zooms in to that little boy's face and the rest of the world blurs around the edges. Of course I know that face. I know that face as well as my own. I've looked at that face every day of my life. At least up until a few years ago, I did. I recognize it now from an old photo album on a shelf in the den at my house. It's the face that grew up to be my father's. "Oh my God!"

"What's the matter?" Vic grabs my elbow to steady me. I must look like I feel—as though I'm being sucked into a tunnel.

"Oh my God!" I say again.

"What is it, honey?"

"You're Victor."

"That's right."

"Victor Caldwell."

"Uh-huh. Do we know each other?"

"No," I say, slumping onto the couch. "We've never met. But you're…you're…" I study at the old man's face. Yes, my father is in there. Why didn't I see it before? The arch of his brow, the almost cleft in his chin, the way his left ear bends. How he bites his lower lip when he's doing something that requires concentration, like when he was scrubbing out the mug in the kitchen. The way he rubs the fingertips of his two hands together when he's making a point. The way he kept clearing his throat when he was talking about his divorce. Oh my God—that was the exact sound of my father telling me he was moving out of the house, that my own parents were separating, and then months later, that they were getting divorced. "You're my…"

"What is it, honey?" he asks.

This must be it—the moment when I finally wake up. Or do I have some sort of contact high from the party? Finding myself in another era is one thing, but this…this is a skew in the whole time warp madness that wallops me. Tidal wave. Is this moment, standing here with my grandfather, the reason I'm here? And if so, what am I supposed to do with it?

"Honey?" he asks again.

"You're my grandfather!" His bushy eyebrows furrow and for a nano-second, I think he recognizes me, too, although he couldn't possibly. "The grandfather I never had!" I say, as if explaining my outburst.

"Thank you," he says. His eyes suddenly get very shiny. He presses against them with the heel of his hands, making an exaggerated face as though he's going to sneeze or something, the way people do when they're trying to prove they're not about to cry. "That's the nicest thing anyone's said to me in a very long time. Maybe ever."

I throw my arms around his neck and cling to him. A moment so charged that it scoops out its own tiny point in time. The two of us. Me and my father's father. I hold him for all the moments he wasn't there to hold me—for when I was a newborn, all wrapped up in the pink, satin-edged blanket that still lives, shredded and stained, in the back of my underwear drawer...for when I was a toddler banging on pots in the kitchen while my mother cooked dinner...for when I was a fourth grader and brought my mother's Aunt Beth to Grandparents' Day... for when I graduated from middle school and was hired for actual money to photograph the after-party. I hold him for every moment he missed, for every moment I missed. I hold him because he is family— my family—a patch of terra firma in the quicksand of these past however many hours, however many days. I hold him because he is my grandfather, and for no other reason than that, because I love him.

He pats me on the back gently. Reluctantly, I let go, struggling to catch my breath. I look at the snapshot I am still clutching in my hand. "Do you have a copy of this picture?" I ask.

"No, don't think so. Why?"

"I thought…I don't know…it inspires me."

"Then you keep it."

"I couldn't."

"I must have the negative filed away somewhere. You keep it. I can print another one."

"But will you? It's important. You have to promise that you will."

"I promise." My mind is reeling, trying to store every little detail about Vic in my brain. He died before I was born; these memories may be all I ever have of him. I'm furious with myself for not ever asking my father more about him, everything about him. I don't even know how he died. I can't tell him to watch your cholesterol or have that weird-shaped mole checked or please fasten your seat belt. I'm so stupid. I never thought much about what or who came before me, and now here I am in the when that came before me and I don't have the information that could change the future even if I might be able to. I'm paying the price for being me, someone obsessed with getting the best grades, going to the best college, being the best everything. I'm not going to lie—it's important to me to be the best so that I can justify feeling different from everyone else, to turn "different from" into "better than." Maybe it's time to be a different me. Be there for the people you love, Vic said. Even if that means having to admit that you love them.

Vic spreads the fingers of both hands, pats their tips together. "Speaking of making prints, I've got yours right here." He picks up an envelope from the coffee table and hands it to me. I sit in silence for a few minutes trying to stop my brain from exploding and sip my tea. The mug has left a damp ring on the financial page of the newspaper where Vic has circled the names of some stocks in red grease pencil. "Sorry," I say, fanning the page dry.

"Don't worry about it. I dabble. Win some, lose more."

"Buy Microsoft," I say.

"Come again?"

"Microsoft. Remember that."

I open the envelope and flip through the pictures. About a third of the way into the stack: there's Jimmy smiling at me. I look at his face. "You're right," I say to Vic.

"Of course I am," he chuckles. "About what?"

"About what matters. Being there for the people... you know..." I get up and give him a hug. "I've got to go."

"I know," winks Vic, tapping Jimmy's face in the photo in my hand.

"I hope you remember me," I say.

"I will," he promises.

"Always," I say. "I mean, always."

He nods. "So do I."

I pick up my backpack from where I tossed it on the coffee table and reach inside. My fingertips land on the pebbly surface of the Leica, its ripples telling a story not yet written. I pull out the camera and hold it in my two hands before extending it to Vic. "It's yours."

"Are you sure you want to part with it?" he asks.

"Yes," I say.

"I don't know...," he says. "Not that I haven't been hankering for this baby, but I got a hunch it's something pretty special to you."

"Please..." I say.

He rummages for his wallet among the Life magazines on the scuffed table next to the couch and starts counting out some bills.

"No," I stop him. "It's a gift."

"No, no, no," he insists. "I couldn't possibly. This is a business transaction, fair and square."

"I can't let you pay for it. I can't," I say. "I tell you what. Consider it a loan. I have a feeling it will find its way back to me." I hold it out to him once again. He looks from the camera to my face and back to the camera.

"I'll take good care of it," he says solemnly.

"I know you will," I say as I hand it to him, our hands touching. I wouldn't be surprised if sparks flew from our fingertips—this could be the moment that sets in motion my portion of some crazy circle of life. Whatever it may be, it's the moment when I'm looking at my grandfather's face and trying to etch it in my mind's eye.

"I'll always remember you," I say. "Forever." And I give him one more hug...in case it's the last.

CHAPTER
23

"PURPLE HAZE?... Orange Sunshine?... All straight from the Bear Man."

I shake my head and take off past the guy hawking acid. I run through the nighttime streets of the Haight, past the head shops, past the throbbing posters in the window of the Print Mint, past the Loveburger joint, past the drifters and the trippers and the searchers.

I burst through the door of the old Victorian, instantly smacked by the smell of toasted cashews and coconut. The house is quiet. I dash to the kitchen and find Jennifer scooping granola off a baking sheet into a mason jar. "You were right about this stuff," she says to me. "The guys love it."

I inhale deeply. Now that's the aroma my mom should go for in her open houses. "You should package it," I say. "You'll make a fortune."

Jennifer shrugs. She's not especially interested in making a fortune.

"Where are the guys?" I ask.

"At that thing at the Fillmore."

"The Battle of the Bands? They went?"

Jennifer crumbles an unwieldy chunk into the jar. "Jimmy finished the song."

"You're kidding! He finished it?"

"Yeah, not long after you left." She smiles at me knowingly. "Imagine that," she adds.

"I have no idea what you mean," I say coyly, like we're in on the same joke, like we're real girlfriends. "Let's go!

"I don't think I should," she says, rubbing circles around her belly. "I'm feeling kind of funny. I'll stay home and make this stuff. What did you call it again?"

"Granola. It's granola. Come on, come with me. Sam will want you there."

⁋

Jennifer and I maneuver through the crowd arm in arm. Strangers reach out to rest a momentary palm on her belly. I want to get her someplace where she can sit down, but that's impossible to find. The place is swarming with a bizarre mix of people—predictably, hippies and flower children in all their finest, but also businessmen types in jackets and ties. We pause at the edge of the dance floor where tables are set up with candy, lollipops, and more apples in the big copper bucket. P.J. stands there, sucking on a lollipop, as he zooms toward the punch line.

"So the guy's breathing his last breath, crawling on his hands and knees when…boom…his head bumps into something. He looks up. Himalaya Restaurant! Holy friggin' shit. It's the Himalaya Restaurant. Specialty of the house...Shlemma Pie."

P.J.'s audience—a couple of guys from another band—nod, wide-eyed. Go on, go on. He's got them.

"With a sudden burst of strength, he gets up and walks in, but he wants to keep it cool, you know. So he sits down and orders a whole meal."

I chuckle. I didn't see that coming. Besides, you've got to love how P.J. is milking it.

"Then...the moment he's been waiting for. The waiter comes over and says, 'Would you care for dessert?' The guy looks up—still real cool and all—and says, 'Yeah, I'll have the Shlemma Pie.' And do you know what happens? That waiter looks at him and says, 'I'm so sorry, sir. We're fresh out of Shlemma Pie.' So the guy says, "Okay, I'll take apple.'"

P.J. holds his breath, waiting, waiting. One of the guys lets out a groan, then bursts out laughing. So does everyone else gathered round. And so do I. There's another unmistakable laugh, too: Jimmy's. He's standing right behind me. We lock eyes, each waiting for the other to speak. For once, it's not me.

"Royce told me you went to that party down on Fulton. He said it was quite the scene."

"I don't know what he told you," I sputter. "I mean, given that guy's overgrown ego and his tendency toward self-aggrandizement verging on the diagnosably narcissistic, it's completely possible that he might have implied that he and I...of course, I don't mean to suggest that anyone, even Royce, would brag about...you know..."

"You're trying to say nothing happened," says Jimmy.

I nod.

"I know that."

"Not just because he's a jerk," I say," but because I..."

Jimmy's not going to fill in the blank for me this time.

"Because I love you," I say.

Jimmy takes my hand and raises it to his face, brushing it across his lips before he kisses my fingers softly.

"Jennifer told me you finished the song," I say, confused.

"*Tamara Moonlight*."

"What?" I ask.

"That's what it's called. '*Tamara Moonlight*'." He pulls a rumpled piece of paper from his pocket: lyrics and chord notations.

"I was named for that song!"

Now Jimmy's confused.

"I mean," I say. Shit, I get it. Finally. You simply cannot tell the future to people from the past. "You named it after me! That's wonderful! That's so wonderful." I throw my arms around his neck, dropping my backpack. The photos spill out of their envelope, scattering everywhere. P.J. gathers them up and rifles through. He waves one under Boo-Boo's nose. "Check it out."

"Looks like an album cover to me," declares Boo-Boo.

"Yeah," says P.J. "if Nina were still around."

"Let me see," says Jimmy, taking them from P.J. He leafs through them, nodding. "Album cover all right."

I study them as Jimmy flips from one to the next. Mr. Chappell would be pretty impressed with one or two if I say so myself. They've got it all: composition, perspective, even really cool interplay of light and shadow. Jimmy keeps shuffling through. Suddenly, I grab his hand, stopping him, before I even know why. "Look at that!" I say.

"Good one," he says, but he doesn't get it. He can't see that it's *the one*.

But it is. It's the picture on the record sleeve in my mom's scrapbook. *Tamara Moonlight*. "Of course! It's you. You're those guys! All of you!" I grab the picture from Jimmy and examine it. There they are: Boo-Boo, Sam, P.J., Jimmy…and Nina.

"Jimmy, we're up after these guys," says Boo-Boo, bouncing on the balls of his feet with excitement.

"We're good," Jimmy says, placing a hand on Boo-Boo's shoulder to calm him. "It's cool."

"You have no idea how good you are," I say. "You're going to have a hit with this song."

"I hope so," says Jimmy.

"I know so," I assure him. "Jimmy, I've got to tell you the truth about me."

"It doesn't matter. Whatever it is, it doesn't matter."

"But it's important."

"Nothing's important except that you're here."

"You don't understand."

"I understand everything I need to," he says. "I thought I was rescuing you. But you rescued me."

I examine the photo again: Jimmy next to Nina. Even if it breaks my heart, there's something undeniably right about how that looks. I rescued him? Not yet.

"When do you go on?" I ask.

"In about twenty."

"Can you switch places with another group?"

"How come?" Jimmy asks.

"I have to go do something. It won't take me more than an hour," I say, "Promise me you'll wait till I get back."

"Where are you going?"

"Just give me the keys to the van."

"Are you serious?" says Jimmy.

"Give them to me," I say. "And promise me you won't go on till I get back." I grab the keys from his hand and then, without asking, I grab the crumpled sheet of paper, too.

"Promise," I say again before heading back through the crowd.

CHAPTER
24

I JUMP into the driver's seat, scoot the seat forward so I can reach the pedals and turn the key in the ignition. The engine sputters, its hiccupping syncopated to the thump-thump of my heart as my palms dampen on the wheel. My hand twitches toward my backpack to grab my phone—muscle memory not yet fully erased. Seems like that's the strongest muscle memory: phone memory. But there is no phone. And no phone means no GPS. There will be no soothing voice to guide me, pronouncing street names with robot phonetics. All I can do is throw the thing into gear and drive. And follow the signs. Within blocks, what felt like a lark that afternoon when Jimmy and I took the van for a joy ride is now something else altogether—grimly serious.

The van chugs up a hill. Why was I so afraid of the flats of Kentfield? They're nothing compared to this. I spot a sign—Golden Gate Bridge—and follow it; the vise at my temples cranks a notch. And then another sign. The signs are coming faster and faster. The bridge must be close.

I stop at a red light—thank God—and roll down the window to gulp the blast of night air. I wipe my palms on my jeans, but can't keep up with the sweat. The light turns green, but I can't lift my foot from the brake. Frozen. Up ahead, on the other side of the intersection—the bridge. The driver behind me taps his horn. But I don't budge. He taps again, then leans on it. I glance into the rearview mirror. The guy's hands fly off the steering wheel in an exaggerated pantomime of exasperation. Other drivers join in. A cacophony of fuck-you honking. Apparently peace-and-love holds no sway in traffic. I step on the gas, but pop the clutch. The van stalls. I check the rearview mirror. A line of cars stretches behind me for what seems like miles. I turn the key. Again. Again. Finally, the engine turns over. I struggle for a deep breath, throw the van in gear and step on the gas. The van lurches forward.

Before I know it, I'm driving on the Golden Gate Bridge. I stare straight ahead, eyes fixed on the car in front of me. No farther than that, no farther, no farther. It's a shiny, new Camaro. I can barely make out the color in the intermittent flashes of the overhead lights: pale yellow. I keep my line of vision tethered to that car. A tassel from a mortarboard dangles from the rearview mirror. Every now and then I notice its silky strands as they swing gently. I try to focus on the strands and on my breathing. No looking to either side, never beyond the white lines on the road that are holding me in and keeping me safe.

Suddenly, I hear singing. *"Somewhere over the rainbow, way up high...There's a land that I heard of once in a lullaby."* Whoa! The sound is coming from me. *"Some day I'll wish upon a star and wake up where the clouds are far behind me..."* I'm singing louder now, in full voice. Singing. While driving.

❧

I've been to the Trident restaurant before. Once, with my dad. Before he left home. I must have been about twelve. It had been a special day, though I didn't know it at the time. One of those father-daughter days we used to have when we took off with no particular destination in mind and laughed at each other's groaner puns and chatted easily about nothing important, because you can do that when you live in the same house with someone and see each other every day. Time doesn't have to be "quality" and conversation doesn't have to be a blitzkrieg of catch-up, zooming desperately from one topic to the next—school, potential colleges, extracurriculars, and God forbid, boys. Nowadays, I can practically see my father ticking off his mental checklist, absolving himself of non-custodial guilt.

Now, as I emerge from the bridge and follow Alexander Avenue into Sausalito, I think about that day at the Trident with my dad. We shared crab cakes and a big bowl of clam chowder on the upstairs deck overlooking the boats bouncing below. Yes, that had been a special day. Remarkable, now, in its sweet insignificance.

Tonight, I can conjure the briny undertaste of the chowder and the slant of the sunlight splitting the waves as they sprayed against the pilings, but I struggle to remember the building. I build one image on the next. Clapboard, I think, and jutting out into the bay, with giant arched windows to take advantage of the view. I have to rely on my questionable sense of direction to get there. I turn onto Bridgeway and hope for the best. Miraculously, it seems that a sense of direction has come with my newfound driving ability, like it's part of some standard package I didn't even know I signed up for. I follow Bridgeway along the waterfront, and there it is. Trident.

Inside, the place is overrun with customers seated beneath a jungle of ferns hanging in macramé planters suspended from the ceiling on beaded cords. The room glows with the light of countless candles on every surface. As for the waitresses—Central Casting must have put out a call for voluptuous earth mother types with curtains of Herbal Essences hair and pneumatic boobs. Note: must be willing to flaunt said boobs, braless, under skimpy halter-tops. Nina must fit right in.

I spot her outside, one hand balancing a tray, the other resting nonchalantly on a customer's shoulder as she chats—flirts, more like it—tableside. I weave through the tables and step out onto the deck.

"I need to talk to you," I say to Nina.

"Well, hello to you, too."

"You have to come with me."

"I happen to be working."

"Listen to me," I say, "you have to come with me right now."

A customer at the table interrupts, "I'll take my Coffee Cooler." I lift a giant schooner of coffee milkshake from Nina's tray and place it in front of him— an overweight middle-aged man with a combover.

"Got a straw?" he asks.

Nina fishes in the pocket of her apron and hands him a straw.

I lift the tray out of Nina's hands and place it in the middle of the table. "I'm so sorry," I say to the diners. "Your waitress has had an emergency."

"Is Jimmy all right?" Nina asks. Of course she does.

"He won't be if you don't come with me. The band's going on in less than an hour. You've got to go on with them."

"They don't need me." Nina hands out dishes off the tray. "And they don't want me."

"They do," I insist. "They really do."

"I asked for extra nutmeg on this," says Comb-Over, surly now that Nina's chest is no longer eye level.

"Give her a break, will you?" I snap at the guy. "Nina, listen to me, whatever you think about me, forget it. This has nothing to do with me. You have to be there tonight. I don't know how else to explain it."

Comb-Over crosses his arms over his chest, waiting to hear how this is going to play out. I smile at Nina, first time ever. I consider telling her about the song and how I know it's going to be a hit, but the whole prescience thing has not proven productive. Besides, I don't have time. "All I can say is…you're in the picture." I usher Nina away from the table, nodding to the diners.

"Enjoy your meal," I say.

Comb-Over's friend leans over and takes a long slurp, uninvited. "Nutmeg gets you high," he says, "doesn't it?"

❧❧

We're halfway across the bridge before I realize that my heartbeat is stunningly regular and there's only a dime-sized patch of dampness gathering in the center of my left palm. I barely need to focus on the car ahead of me. It's almost like I'm a normal driving person.

"We don't have a song, you know," says Nina as we approach the bridge.

"Yes, you do." I take my hand off the two o'clock position on the wheel, dig in my pocket for the crumpled sheet, and hand it over.

"Turn this heap around," says Nina. "This fucking song was written for you."

"That doesn't matter." I'm surprisingly calm. After all, I'm the one behind the wheel.

"You're right, it doesn't, 'cause I'm not going to have anything to do with it. You sing it."

"I can't sing," I say, "but that couldn't be more beside the point. It's a good song. It'll be a great song when you sing it with Jimmy. Wait till you hear how you sound."

"How do you know how I sound?"

"Sometimes you just know something. You and Jimmy sound great together." I can only hope that she knows I'm telling the truth. I'm out of reasons not to.

"Why are you doing this?" Nina asks.

"Because it's obvious," I say. And then I tell her the big truth, the absolute truth—the line I was only rehearsing every time I said it before: "Jimmy thinks you're the heart and soul of the band."

We've made it across the bridge.

And then it dawns on me. I went back and forth over the bridge and stayed in 1967. I thought the Golden Gate was my way back to the future, my present, but not so. I'd been saving the trip across for when I was ready to go home. But it didn't work. I'm stuck here. A few days ago, if you had told me that I'd be whisked away from my regular life, I might not have been so upset. I would have thought improvement would be inevitable. But now, with home irretrievable, I feel nothing like that. Of course, Jimmy is here, but I'm about to deliver Nina to him on a proverbial silver platter.

Nina flattens out the sheet of paper, runs her thumb along the crease to iron it out, and begins to sing softly, feeling her way through the song.

I consider turning around and taking her right back to the restaurant. Let her live the rest of her life flaunting her boobs to Comb-Over guy and guys like him for a hefty tip. I consider pretending to get lost on the way to the Fillmore. Or making her get out of the car right here. Instead, I listen to her sing.

"It's a hit song," I say. "They'll be playing it for years."

AS I TURN onto Geary, the street is bathed in the red light of an ambulance double-parked outside the Fillmore.

"Oh, shit." I squeeze the van into a maybe of a parking spot behind the ambulance. "Come on," I say to Nina, throwing the van into park. "You've got a couple of minutes to get on stage." I bolt from the van. "Come on!"

I grab her by the hand and call to one of the guys hanging around out front. "What's going on?"

"Some chick's having a baby." Oh my God, I shouldn't have made Jennifer come with me. She should be in a nice clean hospital, not having contractions in time to a lava lamp light show.

"Welcome to the Fillmore," says the greeter stationed at the entrance. I "excuse me" my way through the crunch, keeping hold of Nina's hand up the flight of stairs past the ticket hut.

"She's in Neon Dream," I say, with such assurance that the ticket seller nods. We climb to the second floor landing and head for the ballroom beyond.

But a yawp from the tiny office next to the coat checkroom wrenches my attention. Then another, followed by a deep, visceral moan. I glance into the office. It's Jennifer, spread-eagle on the well-worn couch, EMT's crouched at her side. One has a hand on her belly and his eye on his watch.

"You go," I say to Nina. "Just go. I'll be right there."

"But…"

"Just go." I never knew I was so good at giving orders, let alone making people follow them. I step into the office. "You need to go to the hospital," I say.

"No time," says one of the techs.

I kneel next to the couch and take Jennifer's hand. "Are you okay?"

"I'm having a baby," she says in a way that only having a baby can combine panic and elation. And then another animal growl.

"Should I get Sam?"

Jennifer shakes her head no. "Promise. Promise you won't. Let him go on."

I nod. "You're going to be fine. Everything's going to be fine."

"Of course it is," she pants. "I'm having a baby. People…" breath… "do…" breath… "it…" breath… "every day."

"Every day," I echo, though I'm scared for her. Her face slick with sweat, her eyes wide and wild with pain, she looks frighteningly young. How can she be ready for this? For motherhood? Yet, she will be because she will have to be.

"Jennifer," I say, "I want to thank you. I never thanked you, and you're the one who found me in the woods. If it weren't for you, I wouldn't be here."

"You don't..." breath... "know..." breath... "that..."

"Thank you anyway."

"You're welcome," she manages, and squeezes my hand so tightly I feel my knuckles press against each other.

"It's a girl," Jennifer says.

"How do you know?"

"I just do." Jennifer closes her eyes and smiles. "I'm going to name her Tomorrow."

"Tomorrow?"

"Don't you love it? It's so full of possibility." She closes her eyes to ride out a contraction.

"It is," I agree. "You never know what tomorrow is going to bring."

Jennifer opens her eyes and looks into mine. "And we can call her Mari." A reservoir bursts somewhere crazy deep inside me.

"Don't cry," says Jennifer. She sounds exactly like a mom already.

And then I have the freakiest thought. Am I about to watch myself being born? Of course not—I'm too old, too young, all of the above. I kiss Jennifer's forehead as the medical tech instructs her to push with the next contraction.

"Go," Jennifer says to me. "You need to be there. If it weren't for you, the guys wouldn't be here."

I nod. I'll go. "You're going to be a wonderful mother," I say as I head out the door. And my own mother's face floats in front of my eyes, a face I assumed would always be there for me. "The world is built on mothers."

In the ballroom, the guys are setting up to go on. Jimmy straps on his guitar and sets about tuning it. He closes his eyes and cocks his head toward the strings, straining to hear in the din. He runs his fingers through that pesky lock of hair, but it flops immediately, dipping over his eye. He picks the fifth and sixth strings in turn, twists the peg, picks them again.

"Our boy looks scared shitless." It's Royce, suddenly bumping up against me in the crowd. I can hardly hear him above the chatter of people milling around, but the gravel underneath the words is unmistakable. "He should be," he says. "I go on after him. You're sticking around, right?" *Like how could I miss his ground-breaking, star-making performance?*

"I don't think so," I say.

"I get it," says Royce, casting a knowing glance toward the stage where Nina is taking her place at Jimmy's side. Nina says something into Jimmy's ear, explaining how I dragged her here, I'd guess. He looks out beyond the stage; his eyes sweep the audience. I wonder if he's looking for me or sizing up the crowd. Either way, he can't spot me. I'm a speck in the packed no-man's-land of the dance floor, just another girl.

"See you 'round," says Royce, and he swaggers off into the crowd. "Hey, Sunshine," I hear him say to some girl somewhere in the throng—that scrape of a voice.

On stage, Jimmy shoots a look to each of the guys: P.J., Sam, Boo-Boo, then a lingering look at Nina. A look that confirms what I've known all along, whether I wanted to admit it or not—not only is she the heart and soul of the band, but she is Jimmy's heart and soul as well. Suddenly, my own heart cracks, creating a chasm so deep and wide I suspect it will never beat the same.

Boo-Boo counts them down with his sticks, and they break into the intro. Jimmy steps up to the mic and sings. Nina joins him there, clutching the piece of paper. Her voice quavers, a nervous vibrato. Jimmy misses a chord. He steps back from the mic, closes his eyes and takes a deep breath. The guys keep playing, P.J. and Sam buoyed by Boo-Boo's steady beat.

When Jimmy opens his eyes, he scans the crowd again. This time, he finds me—illuminated by multi-colored liquid light; awash in projected shapes without shape; layered with images—mandala over tarot card, saint over Native American chief, flowers over people; absorbed, present, in this collective moment. He finds me. And smiles.

He steps back to the mic. Nina looks to him to bring it. They start the verse again, stronger and without hesitation. Their voices blend in a way that takes even the two of them by surprise. The sound of connection. The crowd is with them, riding the verse to the chorus—compelled by the beat, spellbound by the melody. The crowd bobs in time, then everyone is swaying, then dancing full out. Arms flailing, torsos weaving, hips undulating—yielding to the power of all great songs—utterly unique, yet instantly familiar.

I watch as Jimmy and Nina huddle close at the microphone, but this time my heart does not clench. What a great shot...I reach for the camera around my neck, but it's not there. I don't have it anymore. It's no longer mine. Not yet. All I can do is watch the two of them sing. And dance. So I dance, unabashedly, all by myself. But also along with everyone else. Under the twinkling mirrored ball, I dance like no one is watching.

⋘⋙

WHEN I FINALLY make it outside, a cop is slipping a ticket under the windshield wiper of the van. "You've got to be kidding," I say.

"Red zone, can't park here."

"I stayed too long," I say. "Almost." I climb into the van. I don't really know why, but I have this feeling that finding my way home is a little like a game of Clue. You can't only guess the murderer or the location or the weapon. You need all three: Mrs. Peacock in the library with the candlestick. The van has got to get back to where I found it. I have to be alone. Otherwise, I'd be transporting people to the future and I'm pretty sure that's not in my job description. I sense that there's a third element, but I can't quite put my finger on it. I'm hoping it will come to me as I drive.

The officer taps the van door. "Take it easy," he says. "Better get yourself home. Looks like rain."

And there's the candlestick. Rain.

I pull away from the curb as the mist gathers into a drizzle. By the time I'm on the bridge, it's pouring. The worn wipers are not up to the task. They drag against the windshield, nudging the water from one side to the other. I stare at the road ahead of me, one stretch at a time. And I sing. My song, this time. The song that Jimmy wrote for me. The song my father sang to me in the nightlight darkness. I sing until I'm off the bridge. And then I sing some more. Even as the rain falls so hard it becomes opaque. Even as I follow the signs back to Marin. Even as the road starts to wind and the foliage becomes so dense you can't see through it. I only stop singing when, suddenly, from out of nowhere, a deer appears silhouetted against my headlights no more than a foot in front of me.

CHAPTER
26

"AND THE sun poured in like butterscotch and stuck to all my senses..." What a weird line to pop into my head. My mom's the one who likes Joni Mitchell, not me. But that is exactly how the sun feels. As though it's clinging to my every pore, melting into my muscles, thawing out something deep and long frozen. It's so comforting that for a moment I don't realize that the spot where my forehead meets my skull is throbbing. Nor that *I Love Lucy* is chirping me awake. It takes some time for all that to register. I fumble for my phone. Sixty-two missed calls.

"Hello?" I croak.

It's Sarah. "Holy shit, Mari! I've been trying to get you all night. I knew you'd flake out on the party, you flaker-outer, but then your mom called me, and then your dad, and then your mom and dad on the phone at the same time getting all hysterical. I figured you were probably trying to make some sort of point, but I thought, oh shit, what if something really happened..."

"Sarah..." My fingers find the trail of crusted blood on my cheek. I know where I am. And when I am. I remember the van and the bridge and the rain—the trifecta that got me to the here and now. And I remember everything there and then: the Haight and the house, the band and the music, Vic and Jimmy. My backpack lies at my feet. Rainwater drips off the zipper as I open it and dig inside. At first, my hand finds only my wallet and a hairbrush, but then, my fingers meet the pebbled skin of the Leica. I run my hand over it like a blind person reacquainting themselves with a friend's face.

"Something did happen," I say to Sarah. "Everything happened."

"Are you okay?!"

"I think so," I say, not at all sure that I am. "These people picked me up and...oh my God, Sarah, there was this guy..."

"Oh. My. God."

"I'll tell you all about it later. I have to call my parents." I stumble out of the van—the old, rusted husk with vines snaking around—and phone my mom.

❧❧

I've barely lugged my mangled bike to the side of the road when my parents drive up. They charge out of the car, propelled by a flurry of questions and tears. I suspect the anger will come later; right now they're so amazingly happy to see me. There's talk of the emergency room, but I manage to convince them that I'm okay. Just the same, they study my pupils to see if they're dilated. I'm not sure what they have in mind: head trauma or drugs. Frankly, I'm a little tired of people assuming I'm on drugs, but I guess it's only fitting my parents should wonder; that's sort of the legacy of our newly mutual past, my parents' and mine. Satisfied that my pupils are behaving, my mother feels my forehead for fever, as though it could have been a flu that made me go missing. Then more tears and hugs. My dad trundles the bike into the back of his Range Rover and the three of us—once and always some sort of family—head to a nearby diner. I may have a bump on my head, but I'm famished.

"Starvles the Clown," my dad says, ruffling my hair, because when I was little and got grumpy from hunger, my father would say Starvles the Clown was paying a visit. I can't believe he remembers.

Memory's a funny thing. It's all we really have of the past. But when I was in the past, it was all I had of the future. Once something turns into a memory, it changes. Maybe memory is the one thing with any real power to change what happens to you. Riding in the back seat on the way to the diner, I remember the crack that loving Jimmy left in my heart. It's there still, but it's not going to kill me anymore—it's survivable now. That's how it morphed from the moment when it happened, the moment when I saw Jimmy and Nina lean into the microphone together and I knew with all certainty that they were meant to be together. Memory hasn't exactly made it less painful, but it has made its edges less jagged. It has turned it into a good kind of pain. I never knew there was such a thing, but apparently there is. It's the kind of pain that reminds you that you're alive. That's how I know my time in 1967 wasn't a dream. A dream couldn't transform memories like that. You have to live them first, cracked heart and all. I don't tell my parents any of this, not yet. Instead, I say, "I missed you."

I take the Leica out of my backpack and hang it around my neck. It reminds me of who I am and who I came from. Walking across the diner parking lot between my mom and dad, each of them draping an arm over me, I know this moment isn't a dream either. I'm home for real.

Music drifts from the far side of the parking lot. I pause to listen. All three of us do. Familiar strains from a different lifetime. It's my parents' song. My song, too, in more ways than they'll ever know. My mother and father exchange smiles—relief that I'm okay, but something else, too.

"You go in," I say. "I'll be right there."

They head into the diner, their hands slipping into one another's instinctively, fingers laced together like the pieces of a memory. I watch them walk in. There's a small display in the window of the diner—a pyramid of brown paper bags with a sign that reads:

"We feature Miss Jennifer's Granola—#1 for thirty-five years." A God's-Eye adorns the bags.

I follow the music. It's coming from a jeep convertible, the neck of a guitar sticking out of the passenger seat. I know that back of the head in the driver's seat.

"Jimmy!" I call. It doesn't even occur to me that I might need to recalibrate for the leap ahead in years. "Jimmy!"

The guy turns around. Not Jimmy.

"I'm so sorry," I say. "I thought you were someone else. I know that's a stupid thing to say. People always say that, but I guess it really is sort of a common phenomenon—mistaking someone for someone else. Not to mention the doppelganger possibility... which, given what I've been through, is metaphysical kid's stuff...Anyway, I thought you were..." My voice catches. "Actually, believe it or not, I thought you were the guy who wrote that song. Funny coincidence, huh?"

"Really funny coincidence," says the guy, "because my father wrote that song."

He steps out of the jeep, unfolding his long legs. "I'm James. James Westwood." He runs his fingers through a rogue lock of hair that flops over his eye.

"Mari," I say, "Tamara actually."

"Like the song?"

"Exactly like the song."

"Wow. Another coincidence."

"Exactly."

We stare at each other for a long moment. There's something between us, there's no denying—utterly unique, yet instantly familiar.

"You have your mother's eyes," I say.

"Whoa! You must be a really big fan."

"You have no idea."

We head across the parking lot toward the diner as though it's the most natural thing in the world.

"I like your beads," he says.

My fingers fly to my neck. The love beads are still there. If I needed proof that 1967 was not a dream, I have it. But when I think about it, the beads are no more proof, are no less real, than the crack in my heart.

"I like your T-shirt," I say. I hadn't noticed it until he got out of the car. It reads, "Never settle for apple."

"There's this joke…" he starts to explain.

"I know. I've heard it."

"Wow."

"Hang on one sec," I say. "Do you mind if I take your picture?"

"No, go ahead." He stops and smiles broadly. A natural.

"That's great." I consider the shot. "Actually, I need to get a little closer."

CLICK.

EPILOGUE

MR. CHAPPELL liked that picture a lot, enough to wipe out the Incomplete. He even entered it in a contest. I won second place. The first place winner was a photo of a newborn baby that looked like it captured the very first moment she opened her eyes—the very first moment of her entire life—with way more focus and clarity than a brand new baby is supposed to have, so I couldn't even be that annoyed that I didn't win first place. I like to think it might have been one of the same contests that Vic won, but who knows. I kept the picture pinned to the bulletin board in my dorm room at Yale for three years.

Even after James and I broke up and I moved in with my new boyfriend, Nathan, I kept the picture stuck to the refrigerator with a peace symbol magnet. I had the excuse that it was a prize-winning photograph so therefore deserved to be on display, but Nathan knew better. He could tell that it had some special meaning for me, and he never complained about having my old boyfriend in plain view every single time one of us went for a carton of yogurt. Actually, he was a little proud of it. He'd show it off to people when they'd come over. "That's a picture of Mari's first boyfriend. It won all kinds of prizes." I made a point of correcting him about the "all kinds of"—it was only one prize. But I never corrected him about the "first boyfriend" part. Too complicated. Besides, what was I going to say: "Actually, my first boyfriend was that guy's father?" Nathan put up with me and my entire array of quirks, but he never would have believed that I spent a few days in 1967. Back at Yale, he was getting his PhD in Psychology—I was happy being his girlfriend. I had no intention of becoming a case study.

Even though he's an East Coast blue blood type (I tease him about the III at the end of his name absolutely as much as possible), he followed me to Northern California when I moved back after college. Once a year—well, for the past three years anyway—we drive to Napa Valley and spend a few days bicycling around. Last year, my mom came with us. How weird is that? But she had finally—as in *finally*—kicked old dee-loox Patrick to the curb, and I thought she could use a few days away. At some point I started consciously considering my mother's feelings as though she were a human being apart from being my mother. I was embarrassingly late to that particular revelation. So there we were, tooling around Napa when I spotted a tie-dyed banner stretched across the front of one of the hotels. "Flashback: One Hit Wonders. Tonight." Laying eyes on the thing made my stomach flip, but I knew we had to go.

Quicksilver Messenger Service, Strawberry Alarm Clock, Electric Prunes—they were all there. That is to say, the millennial incarnations of them. There was a lot of gray hair up on that stage, and several extra pounds around the middle camouflaged by guitars strapped in front, but some of the bands weren't bad. I kind of wanted to leave after an hour or so, but my mom said she hadn't had that much fun in eons, so Nathan and I hung in there. Nathan's great that way—really easy-going, which sort of proves the old adage that opposites attract.

We weren't paying much attention to the goings-on by hour three, just laughing and eating tons of upscale festival food—stinky cheeses with crusty bread, salamis studded with pistachio nuts, stuff like that. I was shoving a giant fig in my mouth when I stopped—stopped chewing, stopped talking, stopped breathing. It was the opening chord of a song that stopped me. And then the melody that followed. It was my song. It might have been my parents' song once upon a time, but it was most certainly my song, in more ways than anyone knew. I craned my neck to get a better view of the stage. A big guy with a cowboy hat was blocking my view, so I had to get up and weave through the crowd. But I knew who I would see before I laid eyes on them.

Boo-Boo was on the drums—his hair, more salt than pepper, flying every which way as he bopped his head to the beat. P.J. smiled broadly as he played his bass, as though he hadn't had this much fun in years, decades maybe. It wasn't Sam on lead guitar, but a stranger. How could Sam not be there? Reasons why flooded my brain, including the worst possible reason. Maybe Sam was dead. Death happens. I never really realized that until meeting Vic, but then I got it. My father's best friend since the seventh grade died a few years ago. Dad's eyes still fill with tears whenever he talks about him—which is way more than he used to when he was still alive—and then Dad always takes my face and his hands and says, "Live your life," which, when you think about it, is probably the best and only advice worth anything. And the hardest to follow.

It was too awful to ponder the idea that Sam was done living his life, so I spun a different story for myself to believe, that Sam and Jennifer had moved someplace wonderful, rural and idyllic, to raise Tomorrow. They could be grandparents by now with little Tomorrows running around, Day-After-Tomorrows, as it were, all gathered round their grandmother, Miss Jennifer, as she scoops granola into jars.

No Jimmy. No Nina. My heart squeezed. They couldn't both be gone. Not possible. Then I heard their voices—the unmistakable blending of those two voices into that third voice, the result of their personal alchemy that destined them to be together.

They appeared from the darkened back of the stage, striding forward to the microphones hand in hand. They looked more like themselves than P.J. or Boo-Boo. Maybe staying in love with the same person is a sort of magical youth elixir. Who knows? They didn't separate when they reached the microphones. Instead, they positioned themselves on either side of one of the microphones, the same six inches of space charged between them as the last time I saw them singing together, this very same song, my song. I had cried that night. And I cried again…not for losing Jimmy, but for all he had given me. When it comes right down to it, in his own way, he was constantly trying to tell me the same thing my father always reminded me, "Live your life."

I wandered back through the crowd to my mom and Nathan.

"Where'd you go?" my mother asked. "You almost missed our song."

"I'm here," I said, and I wrapped my arm around my mother, and she wrapped hers around me. Together we listened to the song—my parents' song, my song, our song—swaying to the beat, singing along with the chorus, joyful and full-throated as though no one were listening.

We hung around for a while longer, long enough for the band to join the party. There was one moment when Jimmy caught sight of me through the crowd. His brows furrowed quizzically, his eyes narrowing slightly, as though he were trying to will a fuzzy image into focus. I smiled at him. I couldn't help myself. He stared at me a moment longer, but I turned away, just as the tiniest flicker registered, but before it could sprout into real recognition. I grabbed Nathan's hand, before Jimmy could approach me. *If* Jimmy were going to approach me, what would I say to him anyway, "Remember me from forty years ago?" Hard to pull off when you're twenty-four. Besides, I wasn't sure I wanted to find out if he remembered me. What if he didn't? I wanted to keep my time in 1967 real… even if it wasn't.

The funny thing is, as fate would have it, turns out I'm going to be connected to those days for the rest of my life. On our way to the car, my mother got separated from Nathan and me. By the time we found each other, she had made a new friend: Boo-Boo.

"This is Bob," she said.

"Bob, huh? Wow," I said, extending my hand, "so your name is Bob."

"You look so much like…," he said haltingly.

I knew how he was going to finish that sentence, so I interrupted him. "I look like my mother. I know," I said. "I take that as a compliment."

The rest, as they say, is history. Boo-Boo, a.k.a. Bob, and my mother are getting married next month. She says she's never been so happy in her whole life. I believe her, though I can't forget how happy she looked in that photograph I came upon in that dusty scrapbook—daisy painted on her cheek, eyes slightly closed, kissing my father. That's okay. I'm happy to have custody of that memory if she doesn't need it anymore.

When my parents first got divorced, they told me they were going to be better friends than they were married people. It took a while—and, quite possibly, that bout of shared worry over how I'd gone missing—but ultimately, that turned out to be true. As for me, I guess it took my break-up with James to understand that sometimes you love someone so much you can't contain it, but you know that being together doesn't make either one of you the best possible you.

It's going to be a tiny wedding, my mother and Bob's—just the two of them, Nathan and me, and the judge who's performing the ceremony on a beach not far from the house where the jacarandas still blanket the driveway with their lavender petals. Jimmy and Nina are not going to be there. But I suppose it's possible that some day, at some event, I'll run into Jimmy. I've given it some thought. I plan to say, "Thank you." Musicians are used to hearing that. He'll assume it's for the music, so he won't ask me why. Besides, if he looks into my eyes, he won't have to.

ACKNOWLEDGMENTS

MY THANKS to Marianne Moloney who championed this book from the start, whose enthusiasm never wavered, and who always knows the exact right moment to declare, with great aplomb, "Next!"

Thanks to Alison King for, among other editorial insights, suggesting an epilogue. So glad you did.

To the folks at Rare Bird Books, continued thanks. Tyson Cornell, you had me not quite at "hello," but when you pulled a Rare Bird book from a shelf and proudly showed off the quality of the paper. To Julia Callahan, marketing maven, my thanks.

It has been, and continues to be, a pleasure to work with Scott Busby, a great gentleman of PR, and the WonderWomen of The Busby Group, Jian Huang and Holly Peters. Thanks to you three for your creativity, expertise, and generous indulgence of my techno-challenges.

Beyond thanks to Cami Starkman, who brought her artistry to Instagram, who nudged me toward making the book better, and who fills me with such pride that "our face is absolutely aglow."

Thanks to my husband, Norman Beil, whose unfaltering support took all kinds of exotic shapes: notably making the bed every morning.

This book is also for Laurence Starkman, who grew this story with me, who remembered Edsel, and who wrote all my back pages.

READING GROUP GUIDE

The book opens with an epigraph from the Bob Dylan song "My Back Pages." How does it relate to the story? What would Mari think about those lines? Would the lyrics mean something different to her at the beginning and end of the book?

How would you describe Mari's friendship with Sarah?

What is Mari's attitude toward her schoolmates? Why does she feel this way about them? Is it justified? Do you relate to feeling this way about certain classmates?

Why is Mari's camera so important to her? What do you think about her reaction to receiving an Incomplete in Photography?

How has Mari's parents' divorce affected her? Does she recognize all the repercussions of the divorce?

If Mari hadn't had the bike accident, would she have ended up going to the party with Sarah? What might have happened there? How might the evening have turned out?

How would you react if you discovered you had traveled back in time? Specifically to the Summer of Love, 1967? What would you miss about the present? What would you be happy to do without?

What does Mari mean when she says to the guys in the band, "Can't you see this is just a dream? You're all just dreaming?" And what does it mean when Jimmy answers, "Somebody has to." Which philosophy do you agree with? Can they both be true?

Jimmy says that music changes the world. Do you agree with that? If so, how does music change the world? Did the music of the 1960s change the world? Will today's music change the world?

Discuss the various ways in which Mari is connected to the past without even knowing it.

How does Mari's time in 1967 change her relationship with her parents?

How does Mari's attitude about the concept of the future change during the course of the story?

The title *Shine Until Tomorrow* comes from the Beatles' song "Let It Be." How does the title relate to the story?